NIGHT TRAIN TO MURDER

NIGHT TRAIN TO MURDER

Simon R. Green

This first world edition published 2019
in Great Britain and 2020 in the USA by
SEVERN HOUSE PUBLISHERS LTD of
Eardley House, 4 Uxbridge Street, London W8 7SY.
Trade paperback edition first published
in Great Britain and the USA 2020 by
SEVERN HOUSE PUBLISHERS LTD.

British Library Cataloguing in Publication Data
A CIP catalogue record for this title is available from the British Library.

ISBN-13: 978-0-7278-8917-1 (cased)
ISBN-13: 978-1-78029-664-7 (trade paper)
ISBN-13: 978-1-4483-0362-5 (e-book)

All Severn House titles are printed on acid-free paper.

Severn House Publishers support the Forest Stewardship Council™ [FSC™],
the leading international forest certification organisation.
All our titles that are printed on FSC certified paper carry the FSC logo.

MIX
Paper from
responsible sources
FSC® C013056

Typeset by Palimpsest Book Production Ltd.,
Falkirk, Stirlingshire, Scotland.
Printed and bound in Great Britain by
TJ International, Padstow, Cornwall.

Call me Ishmael. Ishmael Jones.

When people look at all the stars spread out across the night sky, it never occurs to them to wonder if some might be looking back. And the idea that one of them might fall to earth must seem even more unlikely. But not everything in the heavens belongs there, and sometimes the endless dark throws a rebel angel down to earth.

Or, to put it another way, in 1963 an alien starship came howling down from the outer reaches with its superstructure on fire and crashed in an English field. The impact cracked the ship wide open and killed every member of its crew but one. This sole survivor was rewritten by the ship's transformation machines, made human right down to his DNA, so he could pass unnoticed until help arrived. But the machines were damaged in the crash and wiped all memories of who and what I was, before I was human.

I was born an adult, stumbling dazedly across a ploughed field in the middle of nowhere. Help never came, so I had to make my own way in the world, learning how to be human by observing those around me, while hiding from the ones who would kill me for not being one of them.

I might have thought it was all a dream or a delusion, except for the fact that I haven't aged a day since 1963.

Down the years, I've worked for any number of secret and underground groups, because they have the best resources to keep me hidden. I stayed with each group until they started to notice there was something different about me, and then I moved on. Always being careful never to leave a trail.

These days I work for the Organization, solving mysteries of the weird and uncanny, protecting people from all the monsters that walk among them, unseen and unsuspected. Now read on.

ONE

The Man on the Stair

There is a world most people never see.

A hidden world of intelligence agents and secret operatives, psychic assassins and lambs in werewolves' clothing. There are gods and monsters, but there are also those of us whose job it is to keep a lid on them.

Even if the left hand doesn't always know who the right hand is spying on.

I arrived at Paddington railway station late on an autumn evening, with my chosen partner and partner-in-crime, the lovely Penny Belcourt. A black taxicab dropped us off at the top of the steep slope heading down into the station, and I gave the driver a tip nicely calculated to be just big enough that he wouldn't complain, while not so large that he'd remember me. Penny linked her arm through mine and we made our way down to the main concourse. Late as it was, the wide open space was packed with all kinds of people in a hurry to be somewhere else.

I picked a spot well out of the main flow of traffic and looked casually around, taking in the general scene without being too obvious about it. People crowded together before the destination boards, or wandered in and out of the shops, or formed long queues in front of the fast-food outlets, killing time in their various ways . . . and not one of them so much as glanced at anyone else, because, after all, they were British. Every now and again, a recorded announcement would cut through the general clamour, triggering a sudden mass rush for the lucky few.

I couldn't help smiling. I've always had a fondness for crowds. They make such excellent places to hide in.

Penny tugged at my arm to get my attention, and I looked

at her fondly. A slender presence with a sharp face, bright eyes and a flashing smile, Penny was wearing a fashionable two-piece outfit in black-and-white squares, with knee-length white leather boots and a floppy white hat crammed down on her piled-up night-dark hair. Penny and I work well together, solving mysteries and catching killers. I provide the outsider's viewpoint, and she supplies the human touch.

Together, we're a match for anyone, or anything.

'Did we really have to rush across late-night London like mad things, just so we could meet the Colonel here?' said Penny.

'Yes,' I said.

Penny sniffed loudly. 'And he didn't even give you a clue as to what could possibly be so urgent?'

'The Colonel was more tight-lipped than usual,' I admitted. 'He merely stated that we were needed, gave me a time and a meeting place, and then rang off before I could raise any objections. All of which suggests a last-minute emergency, and that once again you and I are about to be dropped in the deep end, without even the loan of a lifejacket.'

Penny sighed. 'I hate these rush jobs. We always end up getting blindsided by something awful we never even see coming.'

'To be fair,' I said. 'That does tend to describe most of our missions. It comes with the job, and the territory.'

'Please don't be reasonable, darling,' said Penny. 'I'm not in the mood.'

The Colonel is the middleman, the man with the message, the only point of contact between me and the Organization. I do know his real name, but I only ever think of him as the Colonel. I've never got on well with authority figures, but as long as he continues to provide me with missions that matter, that allow me to save lives and help protect the world I've made my home, I put up with his military manner and he puts up with my studied insolence.

'Why did we have to get here so early?' said Penny, just to make it clear she held me equally responsible for her current mood. 'The Colonel won't even be here for at least half an hour.'

'I was hoping for an hour's grace,' I said. 'To give me enough time to properly check out his chosen meeting place. But that's London for you. There are those who say the general pace of traffic hasn't changed since the horse-drawn carriage. At least now you don't have to be quite so careful about where you put your feet.'

Penny looked at me. 'You don't trust anyone, do you, Ishmael?'

'No,' I said. 'Apart from you, of course.'

She smiled at me sweetly. 'Nice save, darling.'

'Careful planning and relentless paranoia are what's kept me alive and undetected all these years,' I said. 'I've lived among people for half a century, but I can never allow myself to forget that I'm not one of them.'

'Do you really think they'd be so upset if they ever found out the truth about you?' said Penny. 'People love aliens in movies!'

'Only because they aren't real,' I said. 'Humanity has no idea of some of the appalling things they share their world with, and I'm not going to be the one to break the bad news to them.'

'All right!' said Penny, smiling bravely. 'I shall now look on the bright side! Because one of us has to, and it clearly isn't going to be you. So! A late-night dash through London, to take a mystery train to an unknown destination, with possibly the fate of the entire world resting upon our shoulders! We lead such *romantic* lives, Ishmael.'

I broke off from studying my surroundings to smile at her. 'You and I have very different definitions of that word.'

'But just think of all the strange places we've been, and all the weird things and people we've encountered! I should write up our cases, like Doctor Watson did for Sherlock Holmes. I could always change the names.'

'The Organization would not approve,' I said. 'Anyway, our cases are very definitely stories for which the world is not yet ready.'

Penny nodded reluctantly. 'It would be nice, though . . . to have someone we could talk to, about all the amazing things we've seen and done.'

'We have each other,' I said. 'And that's more than I ever thought I'd have.'

She hit me with her bright smile again. 'You say the sweetest things, darling. Even if I do have to prompt you occasionally.'

And then we both looked round sharply as a VIP came striding through the crowd, barely giving the common people time to get out of his way. You could tell he was important because he was surrounded by a smaller crowd of hard-faced men, there to make sure no one else got anywhere near him. Security guards, with watchful eyes and hands that never strayed far from concealed weapons. The VIP didn't so much as glance at any of the everyday people he barged past. Some of them stopped to stare after him, as though they thought they recognized him from somewhere but weren't sure where. Which suggested a politician, rather than a celebrity.

The real giveaway was the uniformed police officers patrolling the station. They didn't so much as glance at the VIP, or the waves he was making; they were far too busy studying the crowd for potential threats. Only politicians got that level of protection. The VIP reached the ticket barriers and was quickly waved through, bowed on his way by people set in place to ease his passage through the world.

'I'm sure I know that man . . .' said Penny. 'Yes! That's Sir Dennis Gregson.'

'A name that means absolutely nothing to me,' I said.

'Only because you refuse to live in the real world with the rest of us,' said Penny. 'Those of us who actually follow the news could tell you that Sir Dennis is one of those politicians that nobody likes, but somehow keeps on being picked for safe seats. He finally got caught in a scandal some time back; for a while, you couldn't turn on the television without seeing him smiling unconvincingly at a pack of reporters, and saying something evasive.'

'Nothing to do with us, then,' I said. 'Let's go check out the meeting place. Make sure it meets our secret-agent requirements.'

'The Hipster Bar,' said Penny. She shuddered delicately. 'What kind of name is that for a railway café?'

'A pretentious one,' I said. 'Which does not bode well for the kind of dining experience we can expect.'

'Where is it?' said Penny, looking in every direction but the right one.

'Above and behind us,' I said patiently. 'You didn't think I just stopped here by accident, did you?'

'Don't push your luck, sweetie.'

The Hipster Bar stood at the forefront of the level above the main concourse, along with all the classier stores and eating establishments. An escalator led up to the café, but when you wanted to get back down again, you had to use the stairs at the rear. Which was typical of the businesses on the upper level: easy enough to get to, but once they've got your money, they don't give a damn. I stood at the foot of the escalator and considered the café's gleaming exterior. It looked very upmarket – and very up itself. The kind of place that would happily sell you fifty different kinds of coffee, but couldn't manage a single decent snack to go with any of them.

I turned my back on the escalator, to give the crowd one last careful scan. Because something about the station didn't feel right.

'What are you looking for now?' said Penny.

'Crowds fascinate me,' I said. 'Just people being people, leading lives I'll never really understand. Because I'm always on the outside, looking in.'

'After all these years?' said Penny. 'That's sad, Ishmael. Haven't you earned the right to feel human?'

'You were born into your world,' I said. 'I was thrust into it. You grew up to be you, one day at a time; I had to hit the ground running.'

'So you never had a childhood,' said Penny. 'That explains a lot, actually.'

'Everything I know about being one of you, I had to learn by observing other people.'

'How do you think the rest of us manage?' said Penny. 'Honestly, Ishmael, what's brought on this existential crisis all of a sudden?'

'The crowd,' I said. 'People being people so . . . effortlessly.'

'They're just commuters, going home from work.'

'I've often thought I'd like to try a regular nine-to-five job,'

I said wistfully. 'It might help me learn to fit in. I might even enjoy it.'

'You only think that because you've never had one,' said Penny. 'We have something better in our lives; we have *purpose*. Every case we take on is important; everything we do matters. You have no idea how rare and marvellous that is.'

I acknowledged defeat by turning away to study the destination boards. Penny followed my gaze.

'I told you we should have packed a few suitcases. Or at least put on some heavy coats. The Colonel could be sending us anywhere.'

'If we'd needed to pack for a long journey, he would have told me,' I said patiently. 'There's no guarantee we're actually going *anywhere*. We could just be here to meet someone when they arrive. Or intercept them before they can board their train.'

'The Colonel didn't tell you anything about this case?' Penny frowned. 'That's not like him.'

'No, it isn't,' I said. 'Which means that either he couldn't tell me, because no one has told him, or he was told, but didn't want to tell me because he knew I wouldn't approve.'

'You have a devious and suspicious mind,' said Penny.

'Experience is a harsh mistress, and carries a really big stick,' I said solemnly. 'Come on; let's go grace the Hipster Bar with our presence. Make sure it's down to our standards. The Colonel will be here soon.'

The interior of the Hipster Bar turned out to be all gleaming white walls, plastic furniture, and shiny metal surfaces offering distorted reflections. Steam hissed loudly from the over-elaborate coffee-making machinery, while scattered customers perched uncomfortably on their stylized chairs, as though afraid the seats might collapse under them or throw them off. The tables were spindly affairs, that looked as if they might collapse under the weight of more than one coffee cup. There was no sense of good cheer, nothing approaching ambience, and the piped music was just minor hits from the sixties, orchestrated to take all the flavour out. Nothing to encourage anyone to linger, which was probably the point. Just pay your money, drink your overpriced coffee and get the hell out – because there's always another sucker on the way.

The handful of customers sat quietly at their separate tables, staring at their coffee as though they wished it was something else. They weren't there to enjoy themselves, just passing the time till they could be somewhere else. I went over to the brightly shining counter and asked the bored teenage girl on duty for two teas. She looked at me as if I had Tourette's and indicated the board behind her with a sullen jerk of her head. The long list of coffees featured exclusive roasts, strange blends with exotic names and enough additives to make sure you wouldn't sleep for a fortnight. I gave the girl my best hard stare.

'Two standard black coffees. No extras.'

She sneered at me as though I was a barbarian as well as a troublemaker and grudgingly fiddled with the machinery until it reluctantly agreed to dispense two oversized coffees that looked potent enough to rejuvenate a museum full of mummies. She slammed the cardboard cups down on the counter, charged me a small fortune and dared me to say anything about it.

There was a saucer set out for tips. It was empty. I left it that way.

I picked a table at the far end of the café, so Penny and I could sit with our backs to the wall and keep an eye on everyone who came in. None of the other customers seemed to be paying us any attention. I checked all of them surreptitiously, but there was nothing out of the ordinary about them. I sipped my coffee cautiously. I must have had worse, but I'd be hard-pressed to say when. Some kinds of coffee should be declared crimes against humanity. I scowled at the other customers, wondering how they could put up with such bitter disappointments. Penny patted my arm comfortingly.

'Doesn't it wear you out, being so suspicious all the time?'

'People can always surprise you,' I said steadily. 'Even these poor souls, with their tired faces and appalling drinks. Think about it, Penny: what better disguise could there be for a covert operative hiding in plain sight? No one here knows we work for the Organization, and we have no idea who they might be working for. In fact, for all we know, everyone in this place could be some kind of agent, from any number of different organizations, all of them keeping an eye on each other and not even knowing it.'

'You are seriously creeping me out now,' said Penny. She tried her coffee, put the cup down and pushed it firmly away from her. 'All right, then . . . What if some of these people do turn out to be enemy agents? Are we going to have to fight our way out of here?'

'You've been watching far too much television,' I said. 'Fighting is what you do when all your other plans don't work out.'

I broke off as the Colonel strode into the café, back straight and head held high, as though he was slumming it just by being there. A tall distinguished personage in a smart City suit, with an unmistakable ex-military manner, the Colonel was a stern and assured man with cold eyes and a moustache trimmed to within an inch of its life. He didn't even glance at the teenage girl behind the counter as he strode through the tables to join us. He pulled back a chair, inspected it critically and then sat down as though he was doing us a favour. If it bothered him to sit with his back to the door and all the other people, he hid it well. I jumped in before he could say anything. Experience has taught me that if you let the Colonel take the advantage in any conversation, he'll walk right over you.

'Hello, Colonel,' I said. 'You're looking very yourself. I was hoping you might have got over that by now.'

'You haven't changed either, Mr Jones,' said the Colonel. 'Though I never cease to hope that some of Ms Belcourt's better qualities will rub off on you.'

'You're late,' I said.

'It's my meeting,' said the Colonel.

Penny raised her eyes to the heavens. 'Testosterone; I keep hoping they'll come up with a cure.'

'What's the rush, Colonel?' I said flatly. 'Why insist on a meeting at this ungodly hour of the evening, while barely giving us enough time to get across London? What could be so important that you couldn't even hint at it over the phone? And, above all, why did we have to meet here?'

'Don't you like it?' said the Colonel, deliberately ignoring all my other questions.

'What's there to like?' I said. 'It's just another overpriced, soulless tourist trap, that wouldn't recognize good coffee if you put a gun to its head and said, "Look! This is good coffee!"'

'All of which helps to ensure this particular establishment is never crowded,' the Colonel said calmly. 'So you can always be certain of getting a table, with no one sitting close enough to eavesdrop. This is also one of the few places in this entire station where you can hold a civilized conversation without having to shout yourself hoarse just to make yourself heard. Now, if you've quite finished complaining about things that don't matter, we have an urgent case to discuss.'

Penny fixed the Colonel with her best icy stare. 'Why do we always get landed with the last-minute emergencies?'

'Because sometimes that's the job,' said the Colonel.

'And because we have such a high success rate,' I said. 'No good deed goes unpunished. All right, Colonel, I'll bite: why did we have to come to Paddington?'

'You're here because this is where you need to be,' said the Colonel.

'Very zen,' I said.

The Colonel raised an eyebrow. 'I wouldn't know. I have tickets for the both of you on the twenty-two thirty train to Bath Spa, in Somerset. It's a special express, which will not be stopping at any of the usual stations, because for this evening only it will be carrying a very important personage. Though, of course, the other passengers won't know that.'

'Why not?' said Penny.

'Because they don't need to know,' I said. 'They're just camouflage.'

'Exactly,' said the Colonel.

'If we're needed, that means there must be some danger,' said Penny, frowning. 'Shouldn't they be warned?'

'Sending this particular VIP on an ordinary train makes it look as if we're not expecting any problems,' said the Colonel.

'But you are,' said Penny.

'Well, naturally,' said the Colonel. 'Or we wouldn't need you.

The point is, the enemy won't have any reason to expect your level of protection. Which gives us the advantage.'

'What enemy?' I said.

The Colonel shrugged. 'It's not as if there's a shortage. The two of you will travel in the same carriage as the VIP and make sure nothing happens to him along the way. He has his own personal bodyguard, but neither of them has been briefed about you. No one has. You two are to be our ace in the hole – the last line of defence.'

'Unless there's a leak in the Organization,' I said.

'Don't even go there,' said the Colonel.

I looked at him coolly. 'I'm not sure I feel like taking this case. It's not our usual line of work, and you broke protocol, Colonel. You don't get to dictate where we're going to meet.'

'Time is of the essence,' said the Colonel.

That was as close as he was going to come to offering an apology, and both of us knew it. I nodded slightly.

'The Organization is not unreasonable in its demands,' said the Colonel. 'But when you're needed, you take the call. That is the deal you made, in return for the Organization's protection.'

'But what's so important about this case?' said Penny.

'Yes, and why choose us?' I said. 'Any competent field agent could handle something like this.'

'The Organization wanted you,' said the Colonel. 'For its own reasons, which it has not chosen to share with me.'

I sat back in my chair and studied him thoughtfully. When the Organization starts holding back information on a case, that means there's a lot more going on than I'm being told. And if experience has taught me anything, it's that once my masters start taking a special interest in me, it's time to sneak out the back door and sprint for the nearest horizon. Except that I was running out of underground groups to run to . . .

'If everything goes according to plan, you should have a perfectly uneventful journey,' said the Colonel. 'Once the VIP arrives safely at his destination, he is no longer your problem and you are both free to return to London.' He looked at me dispassionately. 'Or are you saying you no longer wish to honour the deal you made with the Organization?'

'No,' I said steadily. 'I'm not saying that. All right: who's the VIP, and why is the Organization so concerned about his safety?'

The Colonel produced a passport-sized photo and set it down carefully on the table. A head-and-shoulders shot of a thin-faced, middle-aged man with jet-black hair, cunning eyes and a pinched mouth.

'This is Sir Dennis Gregson,' said the Colonel.

'Yes! We saw him here earlier,' said Penny, leaning forward for a better look at the photo.

'Giving every indication of being a real pain in the arse,' I said flatly.

'Sir Dennis is a Westminster perennial,' the Colonel said evenly. 'Been around for ages, without distinguishing himself in any useful way. Apart from demonstrating a real skill when it comes to making himself useful to better men, so he can cling on to their coat-tails.'

'He was caught up in some kind of scandal, wasn't he?' said Penny.

'I wouldn't know,' said the Colonel. He made the photo disappear and fixed us both with a steady stare. 'What matters is that Sir Dennis has just been appointed the new Head of the British Psychic Weapons Division.'

'Hold it right there and throw it in reverse,' said Penny. 'Psychics? That's an actual thing?'

'Yes, it is,' I said. I gave the Colonel a hard look. 'How did a political opportunist like Sir Dennis end up in such an important position?'

'The Government moves in mysterious ways,' said the Colonel. 'All you have to do is make sure Sir Dennis arrives safely in Bath. Where he will be met by the Division's security people and escorted to Ministry of Defence Headquarters to receive a full briefing on his new position.'

'But why choose us?' Penny said stubbornly. 'We're all about solving mysteries and investigating the weird stuff; we don't do babysitting.'

A thought occurred to me, and I fixed the Colonel with an amused look.

'Would I be right in assuming there's a shortage of available field agents just at the moment?'

'I really couldn't comment,' said the Colonel.

I looked at Penny. 'That means yes.'

'Everybody go back a step and take a deep breath,' said Penny. 'Because I'm still having trouble with the idea that this country has enough psychics working for it to make up a whole division.'

'Officially, we don't,' said the Colonel. 'But in practice every country has them. Fortunately, they tend to cancel each other out.'

'OK,' I said. 'It's my turn to say *hold it*. Does the Division know we're going to be on the train? Have they asked the Organization for support?'

'Who knows what the Division knows?' said the Colonel, not at all evasively. 'No doubt they will have people watching over the train, from a distance, to protect it from psychic attacks.'

'What's to keep them from reading our minds?' said Penny, darting a glance in my direction.

'The moment they discover you work for the Organization, they'll back right off,' said the Colonel. 'It's all part of inter-agency politesse – playing nicely with each other. Now, the specific reason for your being on this train.' He paused for a moment, to consider his words carefully. 'The Organization has acquired intelligence that an attempt is to be made on Sir Dennis's life, somewhere along the journey. To prevent him from taking up his new post as Head of the Division. Presumably an entirely physical attack, which the psychics wouldn't be able to defend against.'

'Do we get to know the source of this intelligence?' I said.

'No,' said the Colonel.

'Then how can I judge how reliable it is?' I said. 'Come on, Colonel – knowing who's behind the attempt could be a big part of stopping the assassin.'

'If it was relevant, I would have told you,' said the Colonel. 'All I'm authorized to reveal is that this is a reputable source, who has proved accurate in the past.'

'Just how important is Sir Dennis now?' said Penny. 'I mean, are we expected to take a bullet for him?'

'No one's that important,' I said.

'Your orders are to keep Sir Dennis alive, by any means necessary,' the Colonel said sternly.

Penny looked at me. 'Is he about to use the word *expendable?*'

'He wouldn't dare,' I said.

Penny looked sharply at the Colonel, as a new idea hit her.

'Why hasn't the Organization told the Division that we're going to be on the train?'

'Because if there is an attack on Sir Dennis, and we save him, then the Division will owe the Organization,' I said. 'Which is always useful in our line of business.'

'Precisely,' said the Colonel. 'Favours are the currency of espionage.'

'And if we're not needed, then the Division won't need to know about our source,' I said.

'Precisely, again,' said the Colonel. 'Our informant wasn't able to tell us which group or faction is behind the threat. It might even come from inside the Division – from certain vested interests who don't like the idea of someone like Sir Dennis taking over as their new Head. Your mission is simply to watch that man like a hawk until he gets off the train in Bath. Here are your tickets.'

He pushed an envelope across the table to me and then rose unhurriedly to his feet.

'Your train departs in twenty minutes. Please don't miss it.'

'What about backup?' I said. 'In case we have to defend Sir Dennis from an organized attack?'

'You'll be on a moving train, whose driver has strict instructions not to stop for anything,' said the Colonel. 'In the unlikely event of your needing reinforcements . . . you're on your own.'

I had to smile. 'Aren't we always?'

The Colonel just nodded, turned on his heel with military precision and strode out of the café. None of the other customers so much as raised their head to watch him leave. Penny looked at me accusingly.

'You knew about this Psychic Weapons Division?'

'I've heard of it,' I said. 'When you've worked for as many secret groups as I have, you can't help but at least hear about most of the others. Not that you can trust everything you hear.

There's an awful lot of disinformation floating about, partly because no one knows anything for sure, but mostly just to keep everyone off balance. I'd never heard of the Organization until they came looking for me.'

'What do you know about the Division?' said Penny, refusing to be sidetracked. 'Are they going to be annoyed about our crashing their party?'

'All psychics are a bit flaky,' I said. 'Comes with the territory, I suppose. They don't see the world the way the rest of us do, probably because they see so much more of it. As for our unasked-for assistance . . . If we are needed and save the day, you can be sure the Division will be very grateful. If we're needed and we screw it up . . . well, probably best not to think about that.'

Penny frowned, in a way that suggested she was having serious trouble not thinking about it.

'Have you ever met any of these psychics?'

'Of course. All the secret groups use them. They're our equivalent of the canary in a cage that gets taken down a mine to check for bad air. You send a psychic into an unknown situation and then judge how dangerous it is by how upset he gets.'

'But what are psychics like?' said Penny. 'As people?'

'Let me put it this way,' I said. 'You know how cats sometimes sit in front of an empty chair and stare at it wide-eyed until they really weird you out? That's how psychics look at the world.'

Penny frowned. 'Has one ever tried to read your mind?'

'Just the once,' I said. 'We were working a case together, and simply being around me made him act really twitchy. Eventually, he couldn't stand it any longer and tried for a quick peek inside my head. Just the attempt gave him such a fierce headache he had to go and lie down in a darkened room for several hours. I don't know if word got around after that, but no one ever tried again.'

'How can you be sure?' said Penny.

'Because I'd know.'

Penny accepted that, the way she always did when I said things in that particular tone of voice.

'I'm not finding any of this terribly reassuring,' she said. 'Why have you never mentioned psychics before?' 'The subject never came up,' I said. 'Psychic warfare is very hush-hush stuff. No one talks about it, unless they have to.' 'How does psychic warfare work?' 'You've heard about cyber-attacks?' I said patiently. 'How they're going on in the background all the time, but the general public never gets to hear about it until something goes seriously wrong? Same kind of thing. Psychics from all nations, and any number of underground groups, are constantly trying to influence the minds of important people. Or drive them crazy. Or simply give them bad luck. But other psychics are always operating to stop them – from governments or groups protecting their own. It's like . . . a whole bunch of radio stations all broadcasting at once. Nothing gets through because each individual voice gets drowned out in the babble.'

'Is there any way you can tell when psychics are operating?' said Penny. 'I mean, if this is all taking place on some great mental battlefield . . .'

'There are signs you can look for,' I said. 'Psychic fallout. Rains of frogs or mice. Statues that change position, shadows that come and go in empty rooms, fading pleas for help in the middle of phone calls. Look for odd coincidences – like names that rhyme, or two women with identical husbands. It's all just momentary glitches, come and gone in an instant as the universe resets itself.'

'Should we expect a psychic assassin to be travelling on the train with us?' said Penny. 'Is that why the Organization wants us there, as well as a standard bodyguard?'

'Possible, but unlikely,' I said. 'The Division will have its very best people watching over the train. You'd need a really strong mind to get past them.'

'But are there such assassins?' Penny insisted. 'With minds powerful enough to hide them from other psychics, as well as us?'

'Yes,' I said reluctantly. 'A really powerful psychic could walk right past you and you'd never know he was there. Remember the old rhyme – *Yesterday, upon the stair, I met a*

*man who wasn't there. He wasn't there again today, Oh how
I wish he'd go away.'*

Penny shuddered. 'That's creepy!'

'I always thought so.'

'What about you, Ishmael? You always make such a big
deal about your mind being different from everybody else's.
Would you be able to spot someone hiding behind a psychic
shield?'

'I always have in the past,' I said steadily. 'So I have to
wonder if that's why the Organization chose me for this duty
. . . But really, Penny, the odds of us coming up against a
psychic assassin are vanishingly small.'

And then I stopped and looked thoughtfully at the table
next to ours. Penny glanced across at it and then back at me.

'Ishmael? What's wrong? What are you staring at?'

'Something interesting,' I said. 'Tell me, Penny . . . What
do you see when you look at that table?'

She looked again, taking her time. 'Just an empty table,
with two empty chairs . . . The tabletop could use a good
clean, but apart from that . . . Why, Ishmael? Am I missing
something?'

'I would have to say yes,' I said. 'Because I see a man
sitting at that table, looking right at me. And he's smiling.'

Penny's head snapped round. She looked from one chair to
the other, frowning fiercely, before turning back to me.

'Ishmael . . . There's no one sitting there. Really.'

'I watched him walk into the café, right behind the
Colonel,' I said, not taking my eyes off the man at the table.
'No one else looked at him. He didn't stop to order a
coffee from the girl at the counter, just walked right up to the
table next to ours and sat down. I kept half an eye on him all
the time we were talking with the Colonel, just in case he
might be listening in. But now the Colonel has gone and he's
still there, and he still hasn't ordered any coffee . . .'

To her credit, Penny didn't argue, just pushed her chair a
little closer to mine and lowered her voice.

'Ishmael, I can't see a damned thing. What does this
invisible man look like?'

'Small, chubby, surprisingly cheerful – a well-dressed

businessman type,' I said. 'Nothing out of the ordinary about him, except that no one else in the café has even glanced in his direction all the time he's been here. I notice things like that. So . . . I think we have a psychic sitting next to us. One who should stop messing with your head right now, before I decide to go over there and make it clear to him just how discourteous he's being. In a sudden and very violent way.'

'There's no need for violence, Mr Jones,' said the man sitting at the next table.

Penny almost jumped out of her chair. Her jaw dropped and her eyes widened as she pointed wildly at the man smiling politely back at her.

'He's there! I can see him now! Why couldn't I see him before?'

'Because he didn't want you to,' I said, grabbing her arm and pulling it down. 'Now, please, hush, Penny. We don't want to attract any attention, do we? Just sit there quietly, while I have a nice civilized conversation with the sneaky psychic person.'

'They said you'd be able to see me,' said the psychic. 'And I didn't believe them. Most people have no idea I'm around, if I don't let them.'

'I'm not most people,' I said. 'Now get over here and join us, before the other customers start wondering who I'm talking to.'

'As you wish.'

The man got up from his table and sat down opposite Penny and me. He appeared entirely calm and relaxed, and was still smiling cheerfully. And then he sneezed suddenly and looked at us apologetically.

'Sorry about that. The tachyon count must be high. I blame the Martians.'

Penny looked to me, and I shrugged. She peered quickly around the café and then scowled at the psychic.

'How are you keeping everyone else from noticing you?'

'Like you, I work undercover,' said the psychic. 'Only just a little bit more so. They don't see me because I'm telling them no one's here. A kind of selected blindness, if you like. I am the man who walks between raindrops and never needs an umbrella.' He inclined his head to me courteously. 'I have to say I'm very impressed, Mr Jones. You spotted me the moment I came in.'

'It's part of my job – to be able to see the things other people can't,' I said. 'You were listening in on our conversation with the Colonel, so you know what's going on. Would I be right in assuming you represent the Psychic Weapons Division?'

'Of course, Mr Jones. Call me Nemo.'

I winced. 'Must I?'

'You could call me Mr Nemo, if you prefer.'

I looked at Penny. 'He's being clever. Nemo means *no name*. He's saying he's Mr Nobody.'

Penny looked accusingly at the psychic. 'You're the man on the stairs!'

Nemo raised an eyebrow. 'I normally know what's on most people's minds, but I didn't see that one coming.' He turned his attention back to me. 'It would seem some of the rumours about you are true after all, Mr Jones.'

It was my turn to raise an eyebrow. 'There are rumours about me?'

'Only inside our own little community,' said Nemo. 'You know how it is: secret agents gossip like teenage girls during a pregnancy scare. If it helps, no one knows anything about you for sure.'

'That does help,' I said. I smiled reassuringly at Penny. 'I don't care about rumours. Actually, the more the better. They tend to cancel each other out.'

Penny was still glowering suspiciously at Nemo. 'What are you doing here? How did you even know we'd be meeting the Colonel?'

'That's a good question,' I said, fixing Nemo with my best hard stare. 'The Division isn't supposed to know about the Organization's interest in this case.'

'Oh, please,' said Nemo, entirely unperturbed. 'It's part of our job description to know about such things.'

'You followed the Colonel all the way to Paddington behind your invisibility shield, didn't you?' said Penny.

'Might have,' said Nemo. 'Not telling.'

And then he leaned forward, so he could fix each of us in turn with his best intimidating gaze.

'I have been instructed to make it very clear to you that the Division doesn't need or want the Organization's help. Several of our strongest minds will be watching over Sir Dennis's train, all the way to Bath. More than enough to protect against any kind of psychic attack.'

'But there's always the purely physical attack,' I said. 'Even if you knew one was coming, with no onboard presence what could the Division do about it?'

'Sir Dennis has been provided with an armed bodyguard,' said Nemo. 'The Organization's interest and intervention are therefore entirely unnecessary. Not to mention insulting. We are quite capable of protecting our own people.'

'The Organization has good reason to believe that a professional attempt will be made on Sir Dennis's life,' I said steadily. 'And the very fact that I was able to see you, when no one else could, shows I can be useful in ways none of your people can.'

'You're going to insist on forcing your way on to this mission, aren't you?' Nemo said sadly. 'Despite the Division's wishes.'

'I work for the Organization,' I said. 'Not the Division.'

Nemo smiled at me, politely and not at all threateningly. 'I'm sure I could change your mind.'

I smiled back. 'I'm pretty damned sure you couldn't.'

Nemo started to say something, but Penny cut in quickly.

'You even try to put the fluence on Ishmael and I will club you down with the nearest table.'

Nemo looked at her. 'It would appear that the rumours about you are just as true, Ms Belcourt.'

'Oh, they are,' I said. 'Really. You have no idea.'

Nemo frowned suddenly and lowered his head, as though listening to some unheard voice. He shrugged and nodded briskly to me.

'My superiors agree. You are hereby empowered to act as covert protection for Sir Dennis . . . in the event of a purely physical attack. Let us hope you're not needed.'

'By all means,' I said. 'Let's be optimistic.'

We looked at each other, like two fighters who'd studied each other's form and were quietly relieved they weren't going to have to fight after all.

'Is there anything in particular the Division would like us to look out for on the train?' I said carefully.

'Not as far as I know,' said Nemo, just as carefully.

'Then why are you talking to us?' I asked bluntly. 'If the Division really gave a damn about our barging in, they'd make a formal complaint to the Organization. Probably hit them with a plague of boils. Or poltergeists.'

Nemo nodded happily. 'You are, of course, entirely correct, Mr Jones. It's just that . . . We know the Organization exists, but we know so little about it. The opportunity to take a close look at two of its most formidable agents was just too tempting to resist.'

'Hold it,' said Penny. 'We're formidable?'

'Oh, yes,' said Nemo. 'You and Mr Jones have an exemplary track record. For catching killers, if not always protecting their victims. Let us hope you have better luck when it comes to Sir Dennis.' He smiled cheerfully and got to his feet. 'Please, don't get up. Since no one else can see me, that would just look weird.'

'Will we be seeing you again?' said Penny.

'Not if I can help it,' said Nemo.

He adjusted his clothes in a fussy sort of way and then walked unhurriedly out of the café, brushing past people who didn't even know he was there. Penny shook her head slowly.

'All these sudden shocks and surprises are wearing me out. And the mission hasn't even started properly yet. Do you believe all that moonshine about us having a formidable reputation?'

'I don't know,' I said. 'I hope not. That's the kind of thing that gets you noticed. But you can't operate in a community like ours without making some ripples.'

'Like throwing a stone into a pond?' said Penny.

'More like a hand grenade.'

'I don't think I like Mr Nemo knowing about us,' said Penny. 'The Colonel seemed convinced the Division was unaware of our involvement.'

'That was never going to fly for long,' I said thoughtfully. 'The psychics watching over the train would have been bound to identify us the moment we stepped on board. Which leads me to believe . . . that the Colonel wasn't being entirely honest with us.'

'How unusual,' said Penny.

'Well, quite,' I said. 'It's probably all about giving the Division the help they need, without them having to ask for it.'

'My head hurts just from trying to follow all the implications,' said Penny.

'That's psychics for you.' I sipped my coffee and pulled a face. 'OK, that is definitely worse than it was. Could be psychic fallout. You'd better check yours, in case there's a frog in it.'

'How were you able to see Nemo when no one else could?' said Penny, pushing her cup even further away from her.

'Because I've been specially trained. And because I'm me.'

Penny just nodded. 'I was surprised at how normal he seemed. Relatively speaking. Are all psychics like him?'

'Hard to say,' I said. 'It's not often you get to see one in the flesh. Usually, it's just a sudden voice in your head, warning you away from something they don't want you to know about. But basically psychics are just people with an unusual ability.'

Penny grinned. 'I'd love to see one on *Britain's Got Talent*.'

'Has to be better than a performing dog,' I said.

TWO
People Watching

Penny bustled off to WHSmith to buy herself a magazine. She always has to have something to read on a train; I think she's worried her mind will stop working if she doesn't keep it properly occupied.

While she was busy doing that, I checked out the destination boards for the Bath Express. They informed me it would be leaving from Platform 2, along with a flashing sign that said *Boarding*. Just a general hint that everyone concerned should please get their arse in gear and get on the damned train. I checked my watch. Less than ten minutes before the train was due to depart, and still no sign of Penny. I was tempted to go into Smith's after her, but past experience suggested that if I so much as cleared my throat while standing behind her, the whole process would immediately take that much longer.

So I waited patiently outside the newsagents, not even tapping my foot in case that jinxed things, until Penny finally emerged clutching the latest issue of the *Fortean Times*. I took a quick look at the cover: a whole bunch of UFOs hovering curiously over Stonehenge. Penny smiled brightly at me, slipped her arm through mine and chatted happily as I led her quickly across the concourse to Platform 2.

'Sorry, darling, but I simply couldn't find anything I wanted to read. How can there be so many minority-interest magazines? By the time you've reached titles like *Weeding Today* and *What Trowel Monthly*, I think we've passed scraping the bottom of the barrel and headed into the Twilight Zone.'

I checked the contents of the envelope the Colonel had given me, and discovered that we would be travelling in First Class. Well, of course; how else would a Very Important Person travel? But once through the ticket barriers, it quickly became clear that First Class was at the front of the train, which meant the far end of the platform. So I grabbed Penny's hand and went striding down the platform at my fastest pace. Penny made quiet, ladylike sounds of distress as she struggled to keep up.

We reached the First-Class carriage, and a smartly uniformed guard held the door open for us. I pushed Penny on board, took one last glance down the platform and then stepped up into the carriage; the guard slammed the door shut behind me.

Penny and I passed through the vestibule, and the compartment door hissed open before us. Our reserved seats were located right next to the door. Carefully selected by the Colonel, no doubt, so that once Penny and I were in place, no one would be able to enter or leave the compartment without our noticing. I indicated for Penny to take the window seat, so I could cover the aisle. If anything did happen, I wanted to be able to get to it as quickly as possible. Penny sank down into her seat, opened her magazine and then looked at me guiltily.

'Oh, Ishmael, I'm so sorry! I was in such a hurry to find something *I* wanted, I didn't think to get you anything!'

'That's all right,' I said. 'I'd rather concentrate on my surroundings until the job is over. I don't get bored easily, like most people do.'

Anyone else would have taken that as a dig, but Penny knew I only meant what I said. She glanced at the far end of the compartment where Sir Dennis was sitting, and then settled herself comfortably and concentrated on her *Fortean Times*. I looked carefully around me, taking in all the details and memorizing where everything was. Because you never know what might turn out to be important.

The First-Class compartment was brightly lit and comfortably appointed, but stopped a fair distance short of cosy. The seats were widely spaced, allowing me a clear look at everyone, and the central aisle was narrow but uncluttered, with no luggage left lying around for me to trip over if I had to leap into action. And there was enough space between my few fellow passengers and Sir Dennis that I was confident I could get to them before they could get anywhere near him.

I settled back in my seat, and Penny cleared her throat. I looked across at her.

'Have you ever had to solve a case on a train before?' Penny said quietly. 'Given that you prefer to travel by train . . .'

I smiled. Penny always liked to hear about the weirder cases in my past.

'There was the Case of the Missing Carriage,' I said. 'Some years back, a train arrived at Newcastle station with one carriage fewer than it started out with. A whole carriage packed full of people just disappeared somewhere along the route, without anyone noticing. Everyone on the train was interviewed, passengers and staff, and they were all convinced the train had only stopped at the proper stations, and nothing out of the ordinary had happened at any point. But three more carriages vanished without trace, from three different trains on the same line. So the Organization brought me in. This was back when I was working with your Uncle James – the original Colonel.'

'What happened?' said Penny.

'The Organization had the rail company send an empty train along the line, with just the Colonel and me in the middle carriage. It was a bit spooky, sitting there watching the scenery, not knowing whether our carriage would be the one to disappear. We'd put certain defences in place, but even so . . . The journey turned out to be entirely uneventful, but when we arrived at Newcastle, the carriage immediately behind us had disappeared. It took a while to work out what was going on, but eventually we discovered that one particular tunnel had been taking the carriages for itself.'

'How was that possible?' said Penny.

'Because it wasn't really a tunnel,' I said. 'Just something that looked like one. It wasn't marked on any of the official maps; it just appeared out of nowhere one day, settled down in place camouflaged as a tunnel, and went to work.'

'Why was it taking the carriages?'

'It wasn't interested in the carriages; it wanted the passengers. Either because it was hungry or for other reasons best not thought about.'

Penny shook her head slowly. 'What did you do?'

'We sent another empty train along the route, only this time all the carriages had been pumped full of poison gas. That did the job.'

Penny shuddered briefly. 'I don't think I'd ever want to travel on a train again after that.'

'The chances of such a thing happening again would have to be pretty remote,' I said reassuringly.

'But what was it?' said Penny. 'This creature that pretended to be a tunnel?'

'Just a predator, from outside our reality. There are always things trying to get in and get at us. I used to belong to a group that specialized in tracking down such dimensional intrusions, and then shutting them down with extreme prejudice.'

'Is there any underground group you haven't worked for?'

'There must be a few I haven't heard of,' I said.

Penny leaned in closer, lowering her voice further. 'I've been thinking, Ishmael . . . Could there be a psychic travelling with us in this compartment, hidden behind some mental shield and invisible to our eyes?'

I shook my head firmly. 'I'd have spotted the psychic fallout.'

'But would you expect there to be any if the enemy psychic is really powerful?'

'I don't know,' I said, just a bit defensively. 'I don't have that much experience with psychics.'

'You said you'd worked with them!'

'Only occasionally.'

'Like who?' said Penny.

'No one you'd have heard of,' I said.

'Like who, exactly?'

'Lucky Pierre, Fair Weather Frankie, Mad Mental Maggie . . .'

'Those are not real names,' said Penny.

'They're code names,' I said patiently. 'Psychics prefer to hide behind carefully constructed false personas. Like Mr Nobody. The point is, every psychic is always going to be different from every other psychic.'

'So all your vast knowledge about these people is basically useless?' said Penny.

'No,' I said. 'I can still spot one, no matter how many mental shields they put in place. Like Mr Nobody, in the café. Trust me, Penny; there's no psychic hiding anywhere in this compartment. I'd know.'

Penny nodded, reassured, and went back to her magazine. I went back to looking at the other passengers. There were only four of them, apart from Sir Dennis. Three business types – two men and a woman, sitting well apart from each other and working diligently away at their laptops – and the official bodyguard.

The nearest businessman was wearing a suit of elegant cut and style, suggesting he was intent on making a good first impression. His tie had a perfectly square Windsor knot, and the points of the handkerchief protruding from his top pocket looked as if they'd been pressed to within an inch of their lives. He looked to be in his mid-thirties and was handsome enough in a cultivated sort of way. The look of a man who went to a lot of trouble to look as if he hadn't gone to any trouble to look that good. Dark hair, dark eyes, a dimpled chin and a firm mouth.

And yet he couldn't seem to concentrate on his work. He kept looking up from his laptop and staring off into the distance, as though he had something else on his mind. Something he was really looking forward to.

The other businessman, on the other side of the aisle, had to be in his early fifties at least and apparently didn't give a damn what kind of impression he made. His suit was faded and worn, and he'd pulled his tie loose so he could breathe more easily. He had hardly any hair, and his deeply lined face had the lost, defeated look of someone who'd given up fighting his corner because he knew it wouldn't make any difference. He also seemed to keep losing interest in his work. He'd tap in a few words, pause, tap in a few more, and then stop and stare at nothing. Except sometimes he'd look across at Sir Dennis and frown, before looking away again.

The businesswoman was the youngest of the three. An attractive Indian woman in her early twenties, she wore her hair scraped back in a tight bun; her only jewellery was a single nose ring. She worked furiously at her keyboard, frowning hard as she concentrated. Her City suit was sleek but practical, suggesting some kind of junior executive. She had the look of a woman who took her job very seriously.

She stopped typing and looked thoughtfully at Sir Dennis. Perhaps she recognized him from the news or remembered the scandal Penny had alluded to earlier. And then she lowered her eyes and went back to her work with uninterrupted enthusiasm.

I took my first good look at the man I'd been ordered to protect. Sir Dennis appeared to be in his late forties, smartly dressed and impeccably turned-out. His thin, sharp face made me think of a dyspeptic vulture, a resemblance heightened by his fierce eyebrows and receding hairline. He had a nervous, unsettled air, but that was only to be expected now that such a plum job had dropped in his lap.

I thought about who might want him dead . . . A politician who'd spent as much time in the trenches as Sir Dennis would be bound to have made enemies, some of whom had to be killingly jealous of his new appointment. And then there were all the colleagues and rivals who'd had their noses put out of joint because they thought they should have got the job. There's nothing like feeling overlooked and slighted to turn even the most straightforward of minds to thoughts of revenge and retribution. Add to that all the various nations and groups who stood to benefit from the confusion caused by the sudden death of the new Head of the Psychic Weapons Division, and it was a wonder to me that Sir Dennis had actually reached Paddington in one piece.

He was currently working his way through a thick file of papers, with more dogged perseverance than enthusiasm, presumably familiarizing himself with the details of his new job. So he could at least sound as if he knew what he was talking about, when he turned up for his briefing at the Ministry of Defence Headquarters in Bath. Unless his security clearance was a lot higher than his background suggested, a lot of what he was reading had to be coming as one hell of a surprise, but so far he seemed to be taking it all in his stride.

Finally, there was Sir Dennis's bodyguard. A large and imposing figure, he sat stiffly beside his charge, wearing a suit that looked as if he'd tried it on for the very first time that evening. He had the square face and close-cropped hair of a military man, and the look and bearing of someone who could take care of himself, along with anyone else who needed taking care of. His gaze moved steadily back and forth around the carriage, checking for anybody who might pose a threat. I did my best to appear ordinary and harmless.

I studied the bodyguard carefully, trying to work out where he was carrying his gun. There was no obvious bulge under his jacket, but he could have had a weapon tucked into the back of his belt, or even in an ankle holster. His hands were big enough to qualify as lethal weapons in themselves, and he looked like the kind of man who'd enjoy using them.

The train finally moved off in a series of jolts, and I checked my watch. We were departing bang on time. I tensed as the train pulled out of the station, gathering speed. If there had been any attempt at sabotage, a bomb on board or some arranged malfunction, this would be the best time to trigger it. But the train accelerated smoothly away and nothing happened. First hurdle safely passed.

I made myself relax a little. I couldn't keep worrying about every possibility, or I'd wear myself out long before we got to Bath. I shouldn't even be needed, with psychics watching over the train and a bodyguard sitting right next to Sir Dennis. I let my gaze drift casually across the three businesspeople again, just checking to make sure that everything about them was as it should be.

The younger man had given up on his laptop and was staring off into the distance. His mind was definitely on something other than his work. Could he be planning an attack on Sir Dennis? He didn't look particularly dangerous, but then professional killers rarely do. I looked across at the other businessman, who had also lost interest in his laptop. He was frowning into the darkness outside his window, as though considering some difficult decision. Possibly how best to get to Sir Dennis. Except . . . how could he hope to get away with it afterwards? The young businesswoman was almost attacking her laptop, pounding away at the keys as though trying to intimidate them into producing good work. If anyone here had the determination to be an assassin, it would be her.

If there really was a killer in the compartment, these three had to be the most likely suspects. But they all just sat where they were, doing nothing out of the ordinary. God forbid they should make this easy for me.

I looked past Penny, immersed in her magazine, and stared out of the window. Already we were leaving the lights of London behind, and moving on into the darkness of the countryside. Heading through the night like a ship at sea, bringing light into the dark but always taking it with us. Even with my more-than-human vision, it was hard for me to see anything outside the train. Just the occasional lit window in some isolated house, or a flare of headlights from late-night traffic on a country road.

A railway carriage had to be a really difficult location for anyone planning a murder. A brightly lit enclosed space, with little room to manoeuvre, a target almost impossible to get to without being noticed, and no obvious means of escape afterwards. But if the Organization had intelligence that a professional hit was on the cards, then the killer must have worked out some way to get the job done.

How would I get to Sir Dennis? Poison in his food or his drink . . . But the bodyguard would have been briefed about that. A man with a rifle lying in wait, somewhere along our route? No, we were moving too quickly for even the most experienced sniper to be certain of a clear shot, and there wouldn't be time for a second. It was always possible the killer could burst through the door behind me, shoot Sir Dennis, and run back down the train to hide among the other passengers . . .

I looked up sharply as I heard footsteps approaching through the vestibule. I'd just started to turn when the door hissed open and the railway guard came in. A bulky middle-aged fellow in a neat uniform, with a pleasant face and carrying voice.

'All tickets and passes, please! Can I please see all tickets and passes!'

Penny looked up, checked out the guard in his uniform and went back to her magazine. I had the tickets for both of us and handed them over to the guard. He checked their details quickly, while I looked him over. There was nothing about the man to suggest he was anything more than he seemed. He wore his uniform comfortably and performed his duties with the ease of long practice. I kept a careful watch on him anyway. Because what better cover could there be for an assassin than a man with access to everywhere on the train, and what better way to get close to the target?

I'm old enough to remember when a ticket collector would actually punch holes in heavy cardboard tickets, but this guard just scrawled his initials on the flimsy bits of card, handed them back and moved on down the aisle, calling out his refrain with unwavering good cheer. The three businesspeople handed over their tickets with varying levels of preoccupation, barely glancing at the guard. I got the impression he was used to that. He finally stopped before Sir Dennis and his bodyguard, and it seemed to me that his level of politeness increased appreciably. Presumably, he'd been tipped off about Sir Dennis's presence when he boarded the train. The railway company would want a VIP of such stature treated with all due deference.

Sir Dennis didn't look up from his work. He was far too important to deal with everyday details. The bodyguard handed over the tickets. The guard quickly dealt with them and thanked Sir Dennis by name, hoping for a response, but didn't get so much as a grunt in return.

The guard turned around and made his way back down the aisle, easily riding the rocking motions of the carriage. I watched him surreptitiously all the way and listened carefully as the door hissed open and his footsteps retreated back through the vestibule. They were quickly drowned out by the sound of approaching squeaky wheels. The door hissed open again, to reveal a refreshments trolley pushed by a stocky middle-aged woman in a railway uniform, a mess of curly blonde hair crammed under her railway cap. She stopped just inside the door and addressed the quiet carriage with a loud and determinedly cheerful voice.

'Hello, everyone! My name is Dee and I will be your refreshments supervisor for this evening. I can offer you hot drinks and cold snacks! Something to warm the cockles of the heart and reasonably priced treats to comfort the soul of every weary traveller. Ask me for anything! Now, who'd like what?'

She didn't wait for a response, just made her way down the aisle, happily listing the contents of her trolley to each of us in turn until we all felt obliged to order something, if only in self-defence. Penny and I took plastic cups of tea, while two of the three businesspeople preferred coffee. The bodyguard refused anything, for himself and Sir Dennis.

Somewhat to my surprise, Dee all but ignored Sir Dennis in favour of the younger businessman. She stopped her trolley beside his seat and fixed him with her most engaging smile. It was obvious he wasn't interested, but Dee didn't let that stop her.

'Come on, darling, there must be something here I can tempt you with. How about a meat pasty or a nice sandwich? We've got all sorts! You don't want to waste away before you get to Bath. At least have a nice cup of tea and put some colour in your cheeks!'

'No, thank you,' said the businessman. He didn't even look at her. 'I don't need anything.'

'Are you sure, darling? There must be something here you want. How about—'

'I don't need anything!' The young man's voice was starting to rise, and the look he finally shot her was bitingly cold. 'Nothing at all. Thank you.'

Dee shrugged and gave up. She had some trouble manoeuvring her trolley back down the aisle, and I got the feeling she was new to her job. If she didn't learn not to pester people who didn't want anything, she wouldn't get the chance to become old at it.

I studied Dee furtively as she struggled to get all four wheels on her trolley pointing in the same direction. I noticed that she kept her peaked cap pulled well down, half shading her face. Which seemed a little odd for such a determinedly larger-than-life character. I had to wonder whether she might be playing a part, but then why waste the full impact of her character on the businessman and not Sir Dennis? I kept a careful eye on Dee as she backed down the aisle, dragging the recalcitrant trolley after her. And then listened to its squeaking wheels all the way through the vestibule to the next carriage, until I could be sure she wouldn't be coming back.

Penny put down her magazine and leaned in close.

'You've checked out everyone in the carriage, plus the guard and the tea lady. Do you honestly see any of them as a professional assassin? Anyway, how could they hope to get away with anything in a closed carriage, on a train that's not stopping anywhere till it gets to Bath?'

'By making Sir Dennis's death look like an accident,' I said quietly. 'It's the only answer that makes sense. I suppose, theoretically, the assassin could be anywhere on the train . . . anyone who isn't us or Sir Dennis.'

'But you think it's someone in here, don't you?'

'Has to be,' I said flatly. 'It's all about the access . . .'

'Then why didn't the Division advance-book the whole of First Class, so Sir Dennis and his bodyguard could travel alone?' said Penny.

'Because that would attract attention,' I said patiently. 'No one is supposed to know Sir Dennis is travelling on this particular train, remember? They only announced it as a non-stopping express at the last minute.'

Penny nodded and went back to her magazine. She trusted me to notice all the things that escaped her and alert her as and when she was needed. I just wished I had her confidence.

Because another idea had occurred to me. What if there was a psychic assassin travelling on the train, unseen and unsuspected behind a mental shield of invisibility? He could suddenly appear in front of his target, kill Sir Dennis, and then disappear behind his shield again until he could hide among the other passengers. Then all he'd have to do was disembark with everyone else at Bath and disappear forever.

I considered the situation, carefully running through the possibilities. The Division psychics had to be monitoring everyone on the train, looking for just such a mind. But a professional assassin would have allowed for that. He must have a plan in place, something utterly unexpected. The only thing he couldn't have planned for was me.

Anyone else, the psychic could read their mind and be prepared for them, but while I'd never gone head to head with a really top-level psychic before, I was still confident my defences were strong enough to ensure that what was inside my mind remained mine and mine alone.

Back in the nineties, I spent some time with the Alien Trespass Bureau. Checking for dimensional doorways and other unnatural incursions, blocking up holes in reality and boarding over the breaches, and kicking out anything that tried to muscle its way in. The Bureau made sure I was taught some basic psychic disciplines, to protect me from outside influences and attacks. And to make sure the Bureau's enemies couldn't dig their secrets out of my head.

My tutor in the devious arts of psychic self-defence was a wonderfully fey old chap called Sewell, who might have had trouble remembering what he'd had for breakfast that morning, but really knew his stuff when it came to the mental battlefield. He would sit in his favourite armchair, his spindly frame hunched in on itself, knitting furiously as he watched me struggle to master the subtle disciplines he was pounding into my head. It helped that once I had them down, they pretty much worked themselves, running constantly in the back of my mind. Sewell told me I was one of his most gifted students, so I hated to think what the others must have been like.

When we were finally done, he fixed me with his fierce gaze and gave me one last piece of advice.

'Beware the mad minds, my boy, the rogue psychics who think they're better than us just because they were born with a monstrously powerful gift. They have no remorse, no conscience and no restraints, because they believe the rest of us are only here for them to have fun with. They mess with other people's lives, and sow dragon's teeth in the mass subconscious, just because they can. Psychopathic tricksters, giggling in the dark and dancing with the devil. Just for the hell of it. But the really dangerous ones are the ones you never see coming, because they won't let you. So, my boy . . . look for things that aren't there, and listen for things that should be there but aren't. And get the bastards before they can get you.'

Yesterday, upon the stair, I met a man who wasn't there . . .

The hairs stood up on the back of my neck, as though a ghostly hand had brushed across it. I looked around sharply, checking for anything out of place, but the compartment remained stubbornly quiet and ordinary. I calmed myself with slow deep breaths. I had faith in my training. I would know if anyone else was there.

I was sure I'd know.

For the first twenty minutes of the journey, nothing of interest happened. The train roared on through the night, isolated in the darkness, and the people around me concentrated on their work or looked out of the windows, occasionally shifting in their seats as they tried to find a more comfortable position. I kept a watchful but carefully surreptitious eye on all of them.

The younger businessman got up from his seat, and I got ready to get up from mine if he started heading for Sir Dennis. Instead, he just hurried down the aisle and through the door, into the vestibule. I settled back in my seat and listened to the sound of the toilet cubicle door opening and closing, and then locking itself. I couldn't hear what went on inside the cubicle, for which I was grateful. After a while, the toilet door unlocked and slid back, accompanied by the sound of flushing, and the younger businessman came back into the compartment and returned to his seat.

Perhaps a little troubled by the continuing peace and quiet, Penny leaned in close again.

'You know,' she said quietly, 'unless our assassin actually comes running along the carriage roof and crashes in through one of the windows, I don't see how anyone could hope to get to Sir Dennis.'

'Someone must have come up with a workable plan,' I said. 'Or the Organization wouldn't be taking this threat so seriously.'

'At least the bad guys don't know we're here,' said Penny.

'As far as we know,' I said.

And then I looked up sharply, as Sir Dennis's bodyguard heaved himself up out of his seat and stepped into the aisle.

The politician struggled awkwardly out of his window seat, flapping one hand irritably at the bodyguard to give him more room. I looked quickly around the compartment. None of the businesspeople seemed to be paying any particular attention. I focused my hearing on Sir Dennis and his bodyguard as they muttered angrily to each other. The bodyguard was shaking his head sullenly.

'I really should go with you, sir.'

'I'm only going to the toilet!' Sir Dennis said sharply.

'I don't like the idea of your being on your own, sir,' the bodyguard said stubbornly. 'I really think I should be there, to stand guard outside the toilet until you're finished.'

'Absolutely not!' snapped Sir Dennis. He glared at his bodyguard and lowered his voice even further. 'Look, just do as you're told and stay here. I can't . . . do anything if I think someone else is listening. I won't be long!'

The bodyguard nodded reluctantly, and Sir Dennis hurried down the aisle. It was obvious the bodyguard didn't like being overruled but didn't feel he had the authority to insist. The young businesswoman suddenly scrambled up out of her seat and launched herself into the aisle, blocking Sir Dennis's way. He stopped abruptly and scowled at her. The businesswoman smiled determinedly back at him.

'Sir Dennis! If I could just have a quick word . . .'

The bodyguard was already hurrying down the aisle to intervene, and I was getting ready to get to my feet too, but Sir Dennis just fixed the businesswoman with a cold glare.

'Not now! I'm busy!'

He went to dodge past her, but she moved quickly to block his way again.

'I just need to ask you something, Sir Dennis . . .'

'I have nothing to say – to you or anyone else! Now, get out of my way!'

The businesswoman looked past him at the approaching bodyguard and reluctantly stepped aside. Sir Dennis pushed past her and was quickly out of the door. And perhaps only I heard him murmur under his breath, *Nosy little bitch* . . .

The businesswoman sat down and addressed herself to her laptop again. The bodyguard studied her suspiciously as her

fingers flew angrily across the keyboard, and then he went
back to his seat, so he could keep a watchful eye on everyone
while he waited for Sir Dennis to return. I looked at Penny,
who was looking at me. I shrugged, and she went back to her
magazine.

What had been the point of that little confrontation? The
businesswoman had a perfect opportunity to try something,
but she didn't. Politicians had to put up with being recognized,
and sometimes accosted; it was all part of the job. But Sir
Dennis had seemed unusually defensive as well as angry, even
for a man in a hurry to get to the toilet. The businesswoman
knew him, but he didn't seem to know her . . . Did she want
to question Sir Dennis about his new appointment, or warn
him about a threat to his life? But how could she possibly
know about either of those things?

I wondered whether I should go and stand guard outside
the toilet door, just to be on the safe side. I could always
claim to be queuing for the toilet. But that might attract the
bodyguard's attention, and I didn't want to be noticed. Since
there wasn't anything to suggest an actual threat, I just concentrated on listening to Sir Dennis as he fumbled with the toilet
door mechanism. The door finally slid open and he went
inside, locking the door behind him. He should be safe enough,
inside a metal tube with an electronic lock. In fact, this was
probably the safest he'd been since he got on the train. And
then the bodyguard caught my attention. He'd taken out his
mobile phone and was making some kind of report, keeping
his voice so low no one else on the train but me could have
overheard him.

'All quiet, so far. The client is safe and secure. No threats
have presented themselves since we boarded the train. I'll
make contact again when we get to Bath.'

He put his phone away, and I switched my hearing back
to Sir Dennis. It bothered me a little that I couldn't hear
anything, even though I didn't particularly want to know what
he was doing. Time passed and nothing happened, and then
I sat up straight in my seat. I nudged Penny with my elbow.

'Keep an eye on everyone. I'll be back in a minute.'

'What? Ishmael!'

I was up and out of my seat in a moment, through the door and into the vestibule. The toilet door was closed, but the railway guard was knocking on it loudly. He looked round sharply and actually jumped a little as I moved forward to join him.

'What is it?' I said. 'What's happening?'

The guard stepped back from the toilet door. He seemed a little relieved now he had someone else to share his problem with.

'I saw the gentleman go into this cubicle a while ago, sir, but he hasn't emerged yet. It does seem to me that he's been in there rather a long time, and I'm concerned the gentleman might have been taken ill . . .'

I hammered on the toilet door with my fist. There was no response. I called Sir Dennis's name and pressed my ear up against the door, but I couldn't hear anything from inside. I stepped back and looked steadily at the guard.

'I'm security. Here to look after Sir Dennis. Is there any way of opening this door from the outside?'

'I'm Eric Holder, sir, guard on this train. I can override the electronic lock, but I'm not sure I should. If the gentleman is ill, he might not want to be seen being ill, if you follow me, sir . . .'

'Open the door,' I said. 'I'll take responsibility.'

The guard removed a small device from his jacket pocket and fumbled with the controls in a way that suggested he didn't get to use it very often.

'I didn't know these locks could be opened from the outside,' I said.

'We don't advertise the fact, sir. People like to feel secure in the toilet. But I can use this little device to override any electronic system on the train, in an emergency.'

He finally got the thing to work and the lock disengaged. The door slid smoothly to one side, and there was Sir Dennis, sitting on the toilet with his trousers round his ankles, leaning over to one side. And quite definitely dead.

THREE
Who's Been Messing with My Head?

The railway guard stood and stared, and then turned abruptly away, rather than look at what was inside the toilet. He had to swallow hard before he could bring himself to say anything.

'He looks dead. Is he dead?'

'Yes,' I said.

'Was it a heart attack?'

'I don't think so.'

I stepped inside the toilet cubicle, careful not to touch anything, and studied Sir Dennis closely. His neck was twisted round at a really awkward angle, he wasn't breathing, and his eyes were fixed. There was a strong smell of shit and piss, mostly from his trousers, where he'd soiled himself in his last moments. I took hold of Sir Dennis's head with both hands and turned it carefully back and forth. The neck was broken. I let go and stepped back to consider the body again, making sure I hadn't changed its position. That might be important later. There were no defensive wounds, nothing to suggest a struggle, and no signs anywhere in the cubicle that the killer had left anything behind. I turned to look at the guard, who still had his back turned to the toilet.

'This man was murdered, Mr Holder. Someone broke into the toilet, caught Sir Dennis by surprise and broke his neck. You'd better come in here and confirm my findings. You represent the railway.'

The guard shook his head firmly. 'No, sir, I couldn't look at the gentleman. I'm perfectly prepared to take your word for it.'

I stepped out into the vestibule. Given the kind of man Sir Dennis was, I couldn't find it in me to feel much in the way of sorrow. Mostly, I was just angry that the killer had found a way to get past me after all. The guard turned reluctantly back to face me, and I nodded to him brusquely.

'You'd better lock the door again. And put up an *Out of Order* sign. That should be enough, until we get to Bath.'

'Are we going to just leave the gentleman like that? Sitting there, with his trousers . . . I mean, it's not dignified, sir. Not respectful.'

'There's nothing we can do now to help Sir Dennis, except preserve the crime scene,' I said firmly.

The guard nodded jerkily and was careful to keep his eyes on the remote control as he worked it, rather than on the toilet and its contents. The door slid smoothly into place and locked itself.

'Don't inform any of the staff about what's happened,' I said. 'Above all, don't tell the passengers. The last thing we need is a panic on our hands.'

The guard looked at me uncertainly. 'I understand about not upsetting the passengers, sir, but why shouldn't I tell the staff?'

'Because we don't know who might be involved in what happened here,' I said carefully. 'The murderer could have accomplices.'

The guard nodded slowly. 'There are a lot of new people on the train tonight, sir. Taken off other services at the last minute to work this special express. But I'd hate to think any of them could be involved with something like this.' He shuddered suddenly. 'I've never had to deal with a suspicious death before, in all my years on the railway. I'm not even sure what the proper procedures are for dealing with a murder . . .'

'All we have to do is keep a lid on things until we get to Bath,' I said. 'Then the proper authorities can take over.'

'Of course, sir,' said the guard. He nodded quickly, relieved at the thought of Sir Dennis's death being someone else's responsibility. 'Let the professionals handle it. I'd better get back to my passengers.'

I looked at the next carriage along and realized for the first time that all of the lights were out. The entire compartment was dark from end to end. I moved over to the door, and it hissed open obediently. The light from the vestibule didn't travel far, but I could make out enough in the dark to be certain there wasn't a single passenger left in any of the seats. I stepped back, let the door slide shut again and turned to the guard.

'What happened in there? Where is everyone?'

'The lights failed, sir, not long after we left Paddington. Right after I'd finished checking the tickets in First Class. There was no warning, just a sudden blackout. Luckily, it turned out to be only the one carriage. I helped evacuate the passengers and found them all new seats in the rest of the train. Good thing we weren't fully booked tonight. Passengers really don't take kindly to being told they have to stand. I locked off the door at the far end of the carriage, to keep anyone from getting back in.'

'Why would you do that?' I said.

'You don't want passengers stumbling around in the dark, sir, and perhaps injuring themselves. Just because they think they've left something behind. Besides, I needed some peace and quiet in the vestibule so I could concentrate on studying the lighting systems. I've been trying to get them working again, but I'm afraid it's beyond my abilities. I'm a guard, not an electrician.'

'How long have you been in there, working on the lights?' I said.

'Ever since I finished relocating the passengers, sir. I don't like to leave a carriage that way, but I think I'm going to have to.'

'So you were there constantly?' I said. 'No one could have got past you?'

'Oh, no, sir. No one's entered this carriage since I locked it off. Apart from me, of course.'

'Did you lock the end door behind you, after you came through?' I said.

'Of course, sir. I can find my way in the dark – after all my years on the railway, I know these carriages like the back of my hand – but I didn't want to risk a passenger coming in after me and possibly coming to grief. Particularly if it did turn out there was a medical emergency in the toilet.'

He looked at the closed cubicle door and then looked quickly away again. I didn't say anything, because I didn't want the guard to notice the significance of what he'd just said. If the far door of the carriage had been locked all this time, and he was right there in the vestibule to keep an eye on it, then no one could have got to Sir Dennis from that end of the train. Unless . . .

'Did anyone see you working in the vestibule, Eric?'

'Of course, sir. Lots of people.'

I just nodded. That was actually something of a relief. With the darkened carriage acting as a barrier between First Class and the rest of the train, it meant I wouldn't have to look far for my suspect. The killer had to have come from First Class. Even though I would have sworn no one got past me.

It bothered me that I hadn't known about the lights going out in the next carriage. I'd been concentrating so hard on Sir Dennis, and all the other people in First Class, that I hadn't given a thought to the rest of the train. What else might have happened that I didn't know about? I fixed the guard with my best businesslike look.

'Have you experienced any more problems, with the other carriages?'

'No, sir,' the guard said immediately. 'The lights only failed in one carriage. We were lucky there.'

I wasn't so sure about that. It seemed very suspicious to me that the lights only went out in this particular carriage, right next to the toilet in which Sir Dennis had met his death. But how did that help the killer?

'If you'll excuse me, sir,' the guard said hesitantly. 'Now the toilet is secure, I'd better go find that *Out of Order* sign. Oh . . . should I unlock the end door of the empty carriage? If any of the passengers in First Class need to use a toilet, the next nearest cubicle will be on the far side of that door.'

'They can all wait till we get to Bath,' I said flatly. 'It isn't that far. You make sure that door stays locked, and no one gets through from your end of the train.'

'Of course, sir. I'll take another look at the lighting system, but I don't think there's much more I can do.'

He disappeared into the darkness of the empty carriage, making his way quickly down the aisle despite the rocking of the train. I watched him all the way to the far door, and once he'd passed through it, I listened carefully until I heard the lock close. I scowled at the darkness filling the carriage. What did the killer hope to gain by emptying the carriage? No witnesses, presumably. No one to see him approach the First-Class toilet and carry out his commission.

But . . . if the killer had come from First Class, how could he have got to Sir Dennis without being seen? I'd had my eyes on all three businesspeople ever since we left Paddington. Except for when I'd been concentrating on the bodyguard as he was making his report. Even so, no one had passed by me. I was certain of that. The whole thing was simply impossible. Unless there really was a rogue psychic at this end of the train, hiding behind his shield and messing with everyone's heads. Unless that was what I was supposed to think. Could all of this be nothing more than a really clever trick, some cunning piece of misdirection?

When in doubt, start with what's in front of you. I approached the door to the darkened carriage, and it hissed open again. I stepped forward into the gloom and let the door close behind me. The light from the vestibule barely illuminated the first few feet, but I could still make out the rows of empty seats stretching away before me, and the long empty aisle. There was no one else in the carriage; I was sure of that. Even if someone had been hiding, I would have heard something. The only sound was the muted thunder of the wheels on the tracks. I looked carefully around the compartment, and then made my way down the aisle, steadying myself against the rocking of the carriage with a hand on each seat I passed.

I checked each set of seats carefully. Nothing had been left behind, to show the passengers had ever been there. Not a discarded magazine, an empty cup, litter on the floor. The guard had been very thorough. I even took a good sniff of the air, but nothing stood out.

I reached the far end of the carriage and tried the door. It was definitely locked. That simplified things. The last thing I needed was more staff entering the carriage to see what had happened, or to take selfies of themselves outside the toilet. I'd told the guard to keep the news to himself, but it was inevitable that he'd talk to someone, eventually. The best I could hope for was that he'd hold out until we got to Bath.

I made my way back down the empty carriage. Something about it didn't feel right. I didn't like the way the dark seemed to press in around me, oppressive and unnerving. I couldn't shake off a growing conviction that I wasn't alone. I kept glancing around, positive I'd caught some sudden movement on the edge of my vision. I was alone in the carriage; I knew that . . . but I wasn't sure I believed it. I couldn't shake off an uneasy suspicion that the psychic assassin was standing silently in the shadows, watching me from behind his shield of invisibility, defying me to find him. I stopped abruptly and spun around, straining my eyes against the gloom . . . But there was nothing there. Nothing at all.

I didn't move for a long moment, breathing hard, and then I deliberately turned my back on the dark and walked steadily towards the light in the vestibule. I had to trust my abilities and my training, that I would know if someone was trying to hide from me. I needed to believe that I was alone in the carriage, that the murderer, psychic or not, had done his work and moved on. Because if I couldn't be sure of that, I couldn't be sure of anything. I reached the door and turned around, refusing to let myself be hurried. The darkened carriage stared back at me, giving nothing away. I stepped through the door, into the bright, comforting glare of the vestibule, and the door hissed shut behind me, cutting off the darkness and all it contained.

I stood in the vestibule for a long moment, getting my breathing back under control. I was going to have to tell the people in First Class that Sir Dennis was dead, and I needed them to see me as cool and calm and completely in control of the situation. Or I'd never get them to answer my questions. I looked at the toilet door. Not a good way to die, and not a good way to be found, sitting on the throne with your soiled trousers at half-mast. Perhaps that was the point . . . not just to kill the new Head of the Division before he could take up his post, but to humiliate him as well.

To make a statement.

I hadn't taken to Sir Dennis in the short time I'd known

him; even so, he deserved a better end than this. I might have failed to protect him, but I could at least avenge him. I straightened my back, put on my best professional face . . . and went back into First Class.

Once I was back inside the compartment, I glanced quickly around to make sure everyone was still where they had been. The bodyguard sat up straight in his seat when the door opened, expecting to see Sir Dennis, and then looked away again when he saw it was only me. Sir Dennis hadn't been gone long enough for him to be properly worried yet. He wasn't going to react at all well to discovering his client was dead. And I doubted he'd take much comfort from finding out he'd been right all along: that he should have insisted on standing guard outside the toilet until Sir Dennis was finished. Of course, if he had, the killer would probably have dealt with him as well.

None of the three businesspeople so much as glanced at me. The younger of the two men was staring out of the window at nothing, smiling slightly, as though contemplating something pleasant he planned to do when he got to Bath. The other man was staring emptily at his laptop, as though what he saw there depressed him unutterably. The young businesswoman was still pounding away at her keyboard. Whatever she was working on, it had her full attention.

I sat down beside Penny. She looked up from her magazine and saw immediately that something bad had happened. She put the magazine aside and gave me her full attention. I leaned in close, lowered my voice to a level only she could hear, and brought her up to date on everything. Including all my thoughts and suspicions. She listened intently, not interrupting once. When I was done, she sat quietly, thinking hard.

'How could the killer have got to Sir Dennis without us noticing?' she said finally.

'I don't know,' I said. 'I should at least have heard the attack, but I didn't. Unfortunately, I got distracted listening to the bodyguard phoning in a report. I was concentrating so hard on him that anything could have happened outside this carriage and I wouldn't have heard it.'

'Good timing on the part of the killer,' said Penny.

'Suspiciously good,' I said. 'If the killer knew when the bodyguard was supposed to make his call, and planned his attack to coincide with the one time he knew I'd be distracted . . . But then he'd also have to know in advance that I can hear things other people can't.'

'Could the bodyguard have deliberately made that report, in order to distract you?' said Penny. 'Because he's working with the killer?'

'It's possible,' I said. 'Any man can be bought, or pressured, into switching sides. But the bodyguard's not supposed to know we're here.'

'If there's a psychic assassin on this train, how can we be sure what anyone knows?' Penny said darkly.

'Well done,' I said. 'I really needed something else to depress me.'

'You mean apart from the fact that one of the people in this compartment must be the killer?' said Penny. 'And was able to sneak right past us?'

'Unfortunately, it's not even that simple,' I said. 'One or more of these people could be working with the killer, to distract us and confuse the issue. Maybe all of them . . .'

'Just once . . .' Penny said wistfully. 'Just once, I'd like a simple, straightforward case. The butler standing over the dead body with a smoking gun in his hand, shouting, *I did it and I'm glad!* That sort of thing.'

'We don't get the simple cases,' I said. I shook my head tiredly. 'We only had one thing to do: keep Sir Dennis alive for an hour and a half. And we couldn't even manage that. The Organization is not going to be happy with us.'

'Or the Division,' said Penny.

'Exactly. So all that's left to us is to work out who killed Sir Dennis, along with the how and the why, before we get to Bath.'

'How long is that?' said Penny.

'About an hour.'

'Oh, great,' said Penny. 'No pressure, then . . .'

'It's only a deadline,' I said. 'We can do deadlines.'

'Couldn't the authorities just hold all the passengers when we get to Bath?' said Penny. 'Until the Division's psychics have had a chance to take a peek inside everyone's head?'

'Confining that many people in one place would be bound to attract media attention,' I said. 'And then there'd be all kinds of unfortunate questions. The Division can't afford to be dragged into the spotlight.'

'All right,' said Penny. 'Let's concentrate on what we have. Do you believe Sir Dennis was killed by a rogue psychic? The man on the stair who isn't there?'

'The killer broke Sir Dennis's neck,' I said. 'I would have expected a psychic to give him a heart attack, or a cerebral haemorrhage . . . or a dozen other things that would have made his death seem natural. A psychic wouldn't even have needed to enter the toilet to do that.'

'But wouldn't the Division psychics watching over the train have spotted something like that?' said Penny.

'Not if our rogue is really good,' I said. 'Of course, Sir Dennis could have been deliberately killed that way, to make a statement. To humiliate the Division, and show that whichever group is responsible can get to anyone.'

Penny looked quickly around the carriage. 'Could the psychic assassin be in here with us, right now, hiding behind a don't-see-me shield?'

'I think I'd be able to tell,' I said.

Penny looked at me sharply. 'You think? You said you could *always* spot a psychic!'

'But I've never gone up against a really powerful one before,' I said steadily. 'Not many have *and* lived to tell of it. Fortunately for the world, talents of that calibre are extraordinarily rare.'

We sat quietly together for a while, thinking our own thoughts. Finally, Penny shook her head and scowled unhappily.

'Is it wrong of me that I don't feel bad about Sir Dennis's death because I didn't like him? Because I knew the kind of man he was?'

'We can't always protect good guys,' I said. 'He'd been made the new Head of the Psychic Weapons Division; that's all that matters. An attack on Sir Dennis is an attack on the whole country. We have to find his killer.'

'Oh, of course, darling,' said Penny. 'I just wish I could have liked him more.' She thought for a moment. 'You said you searched the darkened carriage. And you didn't see or hear or smell anything out of the ordinary?'

'There was no evidence I could detect,' I said carefully. 'But if we are dealing with a professional killer, I wouldn't expect there to be.'

'Should we contact the Colonel?' said Penny. 'Tell him what's happened?'

'He made it very clear that we're on our own,' I said. 'No backup under any circumstances, remember?'

Penny turned suddenly in her seat, looking at me sharply. 'Ishmael . . . You are sure Sir Dennis is dead? It couldn't just be some mental trick by the psychic?'

'I held his broken neck in my hands,' I said. 'I don't believe I could be fooled that completely.'

Penny subsided, frowning. 'Do you think the Division will blame us, for letting Sir Dennis be killed?'

'Not if we find the murderer before we get to Bath,' I said. 'Once we identify him, the Division can find out who's behind this.'

'How dependable is that railway guard?' said Penny. 'Can we trust him to keep quiet about what's happened?'

'I don't think he'll tell the passengers,' I said. 'But I don't know how long he'll be able to keep himself from sharing the story with someone else on the staff. If only for moral support. Just another reason for us to find the murderer as quickly as possible. We don't want a bunch of well-meaning people turning up here wanting to help, and getting in the way.'

'How bad will it be for the Division, that their new Head has been murdered?' said Penny.

'Strictly speaking, not very,' I said. 'Sir Dennis was just a political appointee, the contact man between the Division and the Government. Easy enough to replace. The point of this attack is to demonstrate to the rest of the world how vulnerable the Division is. In the espionage game, the perception of strength and weakness is everything.'

'The things you know,' Penny said admiringly. She looked down the carriage at the three businesspeople and the bodyguard. All apparently completely unaware that anything had happened.

'If one of them did manage to sneak past us,' Penny said slowly, 'either because they're psychic or through some really clever subterfuge . . . how are we supposed to figure out which of them is the killer?'

'We question them,' I said. 'Work out possible motives, methods, opportunities . . . Eliminate the ones who couldn't possibly have done it, and whoever's left must be the killer. Hopefully, once we've figured out how Sir Dennis was killed, that will help determine who did it.'

Penny looked at me dubiously. 'That kind of detective work isn't really what we do best, Ishmael.'

'Then we'd better learn fast,' I said. 'We only have . . . fifty-six minutes before the train arrives at Bath. If we haven't identified our killer by then, we'll have no choice but to let these people go. And then the killer will just walk away, along with everyone else.'

'Fifty-six minutes, to solve an impossible murder?' said Penny. 'Ishmael, that just isn't enough time!'

I smiled. 'We've had harder cases.'

Penny scowled, thinking it through. 'How are we going to handle it, if they refuse to answer our questions? It's not as if we're the police.'

'If we act like we have the authority to question them, then they'll act like we do,' I said.

'All right,' said Penny. 'We can do this. No, wait, hold it . . . Do the psychics watching over this train know Sir Dennis is dead?'

'Of course,' I said. 'But the Division won't be able to do anything until we get to Bath.'

'But won't they know who killed Sir Dennis?'

'They're only watching for psychic attacks,' I said patiently. 'A purely physical attack wouldn't show up on their radar. That's why the Colonel wanted us here.'

Penny turned away suddenly and looked around the carriage, studying each face in turn. 'Ishmael, I just had a horrible thought. If one of these people really is a psychic assassin, could they have left a mental image of themselves sitting in their seat and then walked right past us to kill Sir Dennis?'

'You're right,' I said. 'That is a horrible thought. And just when I was running out of things to worry about. But it doesn't matter. These people are our main suspects, however they killed Sir Dennis, just because they're here. Unless, of course, that's what we're supposed to think.'

'I hate this case,' said Penny.

FOUR

What's Really Going On

I knew I had to get to my feet and address everyone in the carriage, but I really wasn't looking forward to it. I've never been comfortable doing anything that draws people's attention to me. But needs must when the devil is breathing down your neck and happily reminding you of how much closer Bath is getting with every moment that passes. I took a deep breath and started to lever myself out of my seat, and then stopped as Penny put a staying hand on my arm. I dropped back into my seat, trying not to show how relieved I was at being interrupted, and looked at Penny enquiringly.

'What are you going to say to them?' she said bluntly.

'I'm going to tell them the truth.'

'I was afraid of that,' said Penny. 'You need to tread carefully here, Ishmael. These people aren't used to being part of our world, coping with the kind of things you and I take for granted.'

'You mean psychic assassins?' I said. 'Or just generally the weird and unnatural stuff?'

'I mean murders,' said Penny. 'Most people don't have our experience when it comes to sudden death and unexpected bodies.'

'It's nothing new to one of them,' I said. 'But I will try to be as considerate as I can.'

'That should be worth watching.'

'I can do polite and courteous.'

'News to me,' said Penny.

I got to my feet and cleared my throat loudly, and all heads turned in my direction. They knew immediately from the look on my face that something bad had happened. I gave them all my best reassuring smile, but it didn't seem to help much . . . So I just took a deep breath and dived right in.

'My name is Ishmael Jones, and this is my partner, Penny Belcourt. We're security agents, put on this special express train to keep an eye on things. Unfortunately, I have to tell you that the man who was sitting in this carriage with us, the politician Sir Dennis Gregson, has been murdered.'

I paused for a moment to let that sink in. The passengers murmured *Sir Dennis* and *murder*, and then *security*. *Murder* came as a definite shock, but I could see them turning *security* over in their minds, trying to decide whether that made them feel any safer. I've always found *security* to be a very useful word in fraught situations. It implies Government connections and authority without actually confirming either of them. People tend not to question words like *security*, if only because they're pretty sure they wouldn't like the answers.

I studied the passengers carefully, but their expressions all looked much the same. A mixture of shock, horror, disbelief . . . and a whole lot of confusion. One of them had to be faking it, though. And I really couldn't rule out the possibility that they were all in this together. It might take something like that to pull off whatever trick had allowed someone to sneak right past me without my noticing. I started speaking again, and everyone's gaze snapped back to me.

'Sir Dennis was killed inside the First-Class toilet cubicle,' I said flatly. 'I've had the door locked, to protect the body and preserve the crime scene until we get to Bath. Where the police can take over.'

The bodyguard couldn't stand it any longer. His voice cut across mine, full of anger as well as shock.

'I told him! I told Sir Dennis not to go off on his own, but he wouldn't listen to me!' And then he broke off and looked at me questioningly. 'Wait a minute. How can you be so sure he was murdered?'

'I do have some experience with dead bodies,' I said. 'And given that Sir Dennis's neck was broken while he was sitting in a toilet locked from the inside . . . I'd be hard-pressed to explain how a thing like that could happen naturally.'

The bodyguard slumped back in his seat, scowling hard but staring at nothing. Probably thinking about what his superiors were going to say once they discovered he'd failed to protect the man in his charge. The three businesspeople didn't seem to know how to react. The young Indian woman appeared to be coping best; shock had already been driven off her face by frowning concentration. The older man looked as if he wanted to ask questions but couldn't find the words. The younger man raised his hand tentatively, like a child at school.

'Excuse me, but . . . Can I just ask, who is this Sir Dennis?'

'A politician who'd just been promoted to an important position,' I said. 'His presence is why this service was made into a special express, with no stops along the way. And why he had his own bodyguard.'

'If he was in such danger, shouldn't we have been warned?' said the older businessman.

'No one was supposed to know he was travelling on this train,' I said.

'I want to know why you were assigned to this case!' the bodyguard said forcefully. He fixed me with a cold glare, suspicion filling his face. 'No one told me you were on board. How can I be sure you're the real thing?'

He scrambled quickly out of his seat and into the aisle, and before I could even start to answer him, he bent down and produced a gun from a concealed holster on his right ankle. He aimed the gun at me, arm extended, and even as the other passengers made startled noises and ducked for cover, my first thought was to congratulate myself on correctly guessing where he'd hidden his weapon. I shot Penny a glance to tell her not to move, and then stared unflinchingly back at the bodyguard. Just to make it clear that it would take more than brandishing a frankly undersized gun to unnerve me. The bodyguard raised his voice commandingly, to make sure the other passengers paid attention.

'I'm Brian Mitchell, official bodyguard to Sir Dennis! Military police, plain-clothes. And I am the only protection officer authorized to be here.'

'You're the *official* protection,' I said patiently. 'Penny and I are the unofficial backup. If you're military, you must know how security works, Brian; it's always belt and braces. And never letting the enemy know what the other hand's doing.

Now, please, put the gun down. Opening fire in a confined space is rarely a good idea.'

'Oh, you'd like that, wouldn't you?' said Brian, trying to sound as though he was in charge and missing by a mile.

'Yes, I would like that,' I said. 'I'm sure everyone here would feel a lot safer if no one was waving a gun around.'

'I am not waving it around!' Brian said loudly.

He took a step forward and aimed the gun right between my eyes, as though that would make it more threatening. When I just stared calmly back at him, he turned the gun away from me and aimed it at Penny, thinking I'd be more concerned for her than I was for my own safety. And I decided that enough was enough. I charged down the aisle toward him, and he automatically started to turn the gun back to me, but by then I was right on top of him. I snatched the gun out of his hand, turned it around and took careful aim at his heart. He looked at me with shocked eyes, started to raise his hands and then stopped, for fear I might take that as a threat. I took a step back, lowered the gun and put it away in my jacket pocket.

'Calm the hell down, Brian,' I said. 'We've already got one body on this train; let's not try for two.'

Brian had to open and shut his mouth a few times before he felt able to answer me.

'Give me back my gun! I had to sign for that.'

'Maybe later,' I said. 'Now, sit down and behave yourself.'

He thought about arguing, thought better of it and sat down in his seat again, scowling at me like a child who'd just had his favourite toy taken away. I turned to the three business-people, who were slowly sitting up in their seats again. They all looked a bit stunned. They weren't used to guns, and they'd never seen anyone disarm a man so easily. I tried my reassuring smile again.

'It's all in the reflexes.'

The three of them thought about that and actually relaxed a little. What I'd just given them was one of those answers that doesn't actually mean anything but sounds as though it does. Something to reassure people into thinking they've received an explanation when they really haven't. I noticed the young Indian woman was keeping a wary eye on the jacket pocket where I'd put the gun.

'I still want to know why I wasn't told about you,' Brian said stubbornly.

'Because you didn't need to know,' I said. 'Penny and I were brought in at the last minute, as an extra level of protection.'

'They didn't trust me,' Brian said bitterly. 'I was never really Sir Dennis's bodyguard . . . I was just a decoy, a distraction, someone to hold the killer's attention while you did the real job. Well, the joke's on you, Mr Jones, because in the end you were no more use than I was.'

The younger businessman raised his hand again.

'You don't need to do that,' I said patiently. 'Just introduce yourself and ask your question.'

'Oh, right. I'm Rupert Hall. Are you planning to stop the train before we get to Bath?'

'I'm Sita Patel,' the Indian woman said immediately. 'What's the point in stopping the train? Sir Dennis is dead; stopping won't change anything.'

'I've arranged to meet someone in Bath,' said Rupert. 'And I really don't want to be late.'

'I'm sure they'll wait for you,' said Sita. 'There's been a murder; try to concentrate on what matters.'

Rupert looked quietly crushed and subsided back into his seat in the face of Sita's open disdain.

'I'm Howard Goldwasser,' said the older of the businessmen. 'Aren't we supposed to pull the communication cord? Isn't that the correct thing to do in this situation?'

'This is a special express,' said Brian, trying to grab back some of his authority. 'The driver is under strict instructions not to stop for anything until we get to Bath.'

'Even though a man is dead?' said Sita.

'Especially now he's dead,' I said.

Sita frowned and seemed to lose some of her assurance. 'I thought we'd be stopping at the next station.'

Brian smiled. 'Think again.'

'I wasn't told anything about this being a special express,' said Howard.

'Then you should have paid more attention,' said Brian.

'The authorities will be waiting to meet us at Bath,' I said, keeping my voice carefully calm and reasonable. 'Brian, you and I need to talk. Penny, why don't you have a nice little chat with the rest of the passengers? Bring them up to speed on what's happened, and answer any questions they may have.'

Penny gestured for me to lean in close. 'How much should I tell them?' she asked quietly.

'As little as possible,' I said, just as quietly. 'Calm them down and keep them quiet, while I question the bodyguard.'

'Thanks a bunch,' said Penny.

'Would you rather talk to the bodyguard?'

'I'll talk to the passengers.'

Penny got up out of her seat, all smiles and charm, and quickly persuaded the three businesspeople that they should all move further down the carriage and sit together. Penny's always been good at persuading people to do what she wants. I've never really had the knack. I sat down opposite the bodyguard, and he scowled sullenly at me.

'When am I going to get my gun back?'

'When I think you can be trusted with it,' I said. We locked eyes for a moment, and although he didn't look away, he did lose some of his belligerence. He sat back in his seat and studied me suspiciously.

'All right, what is it you want to talk about, Mr Jones? Is that really your name – Ishmael Jones?'

'You know how it is,' I said. 'You take what you're given. Now, we need to figure out how Sir Dennis was killed.'

'I can't tell you anything,' said Brian. 'Sir Dennis was fine all the time he was with me. A complete pain in the arse, but fine. Then he decided he had to go to the toilet; the next thing I know, you're telling me the man is dead.'

'Someone must have broken into the toilet cubicle, killed Sir Dennis and somehow locked the door again when they left,' I said. 'All without anyone noticing. I couldn't find a single clue to indicate who did it, but I do have good reason to believe the killer is someone in this carriage.'

Brian sat up sharply and peered down the compartment at

the other passengers. 'Oh, come on! Those three? There's not one of them looks like a killer.'

'Killers rarely do,' I said.

'But . . . I was sitting right here, looking down the aisle and waiting for Sir Dennis to come back,' said Brian. He frowned, concentrating. 'No one left the compartment after he did; I couldn't have missed seeing them. The killer must have come from somewhere further down the train.'

'That's not possible,' I said. 'The next carriage along had to be evacuated soon after we left Paddington, when all the lights failed. The door at the far end of that carriage has been locked and guarded ever since. No one could have come through from that end.'

'But . . . that's just not possible!' said Brian. 'Even if I had taken my eyes off the aisle for a moment, you and the girl were sitting right next to the door. You couldn't have avoided seeing anyone go past you.'

'Intriguing, isn't it?' I said. 'Not to mention patently impossible. But someone must have managed it.'

'All right,' said Brian. 'I give up. What's the answer?'

'Damned if I know,' I said. 'You stay here and think about it, while I go and have a word with the other passengers.'

'You don't want me to come with you?'

'One set of questions at a time, I think,' I said diplomatically.

'Don't take any nonsense from them,' Brian said flatly. 'In my experience, the best way to get answers out of people is to just keep hammering away at them until they crack.'

'I'll bear that in mind,' I said. I got to my feet.

'Hey!' said Brian. 'What about my gun?'

I looked back at him as I stepped out into the aisle. 'What about it?'

I left him still trying to come up with an answer to that one and went to join Penny and the businesspeople. She saw me coming and got up to join me halfway. We stood close together and lowered our voices.

'Are you going to give that man his gun back?' said Penny.

'Not if I can help it,' I said. 'The last thing we need right now is a gun in the hand of someone with serious impulse control problems. How are the others taking things?'

'Confused, mostly,' said Penny. 'Along with shocked, upset and very worried about what's going to happen to them. The general consensus seems to be that they don't know anything about what happened to Sir Dennis, and they don't want to know. It's nothing to do with them, so would we please just leave them alone.'

'Sita Patel knew who Sir Dennis was,' I said. 'She tried to ask him questions on the way to the toilet. He had to barge past her, pretty unpleasantly. I would really like to know what it was she wanted to ask him. And I saw Howard Goldwasser look at Sir Dennis more than once. He knew who the man was – and not in a good way. Were you able to get anything out of Rupert Hall?'

'Not really. He just keeps insisting he has to meet someone in Bath and doesn't want to be late.'

'Business or personal?'

'He wouldn't say.'

'I'd better talk to them,' I said. 'They must know something about what happened, even if they don't realize it.'

'What are you going to ask them?' Penny said cautiously.

'I don't know,' I said. 'Anything that comes to mind. Right now, we don't know a damned thing about them or the murder. Any information has to be better than none.'

We went back to the three businesspeople. They seemed happy enough to see Penny again, less so when it came to me. I was used to that. Instead of sitting down, I stood towering over them, for the extra authority it gave me.

'I know this has been a shock and a strain for all of you,' I said. 'Please try to stay calm and let us do our job.'

'What is your job, exactly?' Sita said immediately.

'Finding out who killed Sir Dennis,' I said.

'Shouldn't you be showing us some ID?' said Sita. 'Something to prove you really are who you say you are. You could be anybody!'

'People like us don't carry ID,' said Penny.

Strangely, that seemed to reassure them. It made us seem more like the real thing than any form of ID could have managed. If you ask me, people watch far too many spy shows on television.

'There's no point asking us questions,' said Rupert. His voice was surprisingly diffident for such a well-built man, and he had trouble making eye contact with me. 'We don't know anything about this politician or how he was killed.'

'People often say that,' I said. 'But you'd be surprised how much you do notice without realizing.'

'Are you going to interrogate us?' said Sita.

'Just ask a few questions,' I said.

'I didn't see or hear anything,' Howard said flatly, and the other two nodded quickly in agreement.

'Then the questioning shouldn't take too long, should it?' I said pleasantly. 'For now, just sit tight and think about what you're going to say, while I nip back and have another quick chat with the bodyguard.'

I gestured to Penny, and we moved back down the aisle again.

'Let them stew for a few minutes, and then I'll try again,' I said.

'What if they really don't know anything?' said Penny.

'One of them must,' I said. 'You keep them entertained, while I try to dig some more information out of the bodyguard.'

'Keep them entertained?' said Penny, just a bit dangerously. 'What am I, your social secretary?'

'You are my valued partner,' I said. 'Which is why I feel perfectly safe leaving three potential murder suspects in your care. It's always possible that they'll feel relaxed enough in your company to tell you things, rather than face my inter-rogation. Because you're the nice one.'

'Well,' said Penny, 'that goes without saying.'

I went back to Brian and sat down opposite him again. He folded his arms and sniffed loudly.

'What do you want now, security man?'

'How did you get the job as Sir Dennis's bodyguard?' I said. 'You said you were military police . . .'

'Shouldn't you already know that?'

'Penny and I were only brought on to this case at the last moment,' I said patiently. 'There wasn't time for a proper briefing.'

Brian allowed himself a small smile. 'Isn't that always the

way? All right . . . I'm a military police officer, attached to the strength at Woolwich Arsenal. Half a dozen of us were summoned before our commanding officer earlier this evening and told we were being considered for an important assignment. Extra money was mentioned, along with improved career prospects, which, of course, made all of us very suspicious. Never volunteer for anything in the army. But it was also made clear to us that declining this marvellous opportunity wasn't going to be an option. So we drew straws, and I got the job.

'When they explained what was involved, it all sounded simple enough . . . but now I just know I'm going to get the blame for letting Sir Dennis go off on his own and get killed. All I had to do was watch the man, and I blew it. He was only out of my sight for a few minutes!'

'Sometimes that's all it takes,' I said. 'But you're in the clear, Brian; I heard him order you to stay put.'

'Well,' said Brian, 'that's something. If he'd only paid proper attention to my advice, he'd still be alive. But he wouldn't listen . . . The arrogant little creep.' He stopped and looked at me steadily. 'Give it to me straight. Why did the powers that be think they needed you here, as well as me?'

'My people received advance information that someone was planning a professional hit,' I said.

'I was bait, wasn't I?' Brian said quietly. 'Just a warm body for the hitman to deal with on his way to Sir Dennis, so you could take them down.' He smiled a smile with no humour in it. 'That's the army for you. Use you up and throw you away, because there's always more waiting to be used.'

'You don't seem too surprised, or even upset, about that,' I said.

He shrugged. 'Any soldier worth his salt works that one out quickly enough. It's all part of the deal, from the moment you sign up. You give your life to the army so you can protect your country, and they get to decide what to do with it.' He nodded suddenly, as though he'd just come to a decision. 'You know what? You and what's-her-name can run this investigation without me. I know when I'm out of my depth. But I expect to be kept in the loop, if you find out anything.'

'I'll tell you what I can,' I said.

I might or I might not, but I was pretty sure Brian already understood that. We were both just going through the courtesies, for our pride's sake. I can do people skills, when I have to.

'Whatever questions you have left for me, let's get them out of the way now,' said Brian. 'So you can concentrate on the real suspects. No, wait a minute! I thought of something while you were off talking to the others . . . Could the killer still be hiding somewhere in the space between the carriages? Tucked away in some hidden compartment? I saw this movie once where a midget curled himself up in a space so small you wouldn't believe it . . .'

'I really don't think so,' I said.

'Aren't you at least going to take a look?'

'There's nowhere in the vestibule that anyone could be hiding,' I said firmly.

I could be sure of that because I would have heard their heartbeat or picked up on their scent but, of course, I couldn't tell Brian that. He looked disappointed but nodded reluctantly.

'Talk to me about Sir Dennis,' I said. 'You spent more time talking with him than anyone else.'

'It's not like we were close,' he said. He seemed to find the idea amusing. 'As far as he was concerned, I was just a bullet-proof vest on legs. Something he could hide behind if the bullets started flying.'

'Did he mention his new job?' I said. 'Or anyone he might have upset recently, who he had reason to be concerned about? There's always the chance the motive for his murder could turn out to be personal, rather than political.'

'You can rule me out either way,' said Brian. 'I was chosen by lot just to ensure I wouldn't have any connection to the man. Once I'd got the job, they just gave me a suit and gun and drove me straight to the station.'

'All right,' I said. 'What did the two of you find to talk about?'

Brian scowled. 'Sir Dennis wasn't interested in anything I had to say; he just wanted to boast about his new position and how important that made him. He was so full of himself he had to tell someone, and I was all he had.' His frown deepened. 'I got the impression this new appointment came as something of a surprise. He hadn't gone after it, never thought he stood a chance. So when it just fell into his lap, he was convinced it meant the beginning of a whole new career for him. And he was going to ride it as far as it would take him.'

'Sir Dennis had a big file with him,' I said. 'Did he discuss its contents at all?'

'Not a word,' Brian said immediately. 'Wouldn't even let me look at it. Said my security clearance wasn't high enough. Really, I think it was just something else he could use to lord it over me.'

'Where's the file now?'

'While you were off talking to the others, I stowed it in the luggage rack,' said Brian. 'Out of everyone's way. That seemed safest.'

I looked to where he pointed, and nodded. It was safe enough there, well out of reach.

'So you didn't even know what his new appointment was?'

'I didn't need to know,' Brian said flatly. 'My job was just to get the man safely to Bath. And I would have, if he hadn't been such a wimp about using a public toilet. None of what's happened is my fault!'

'I'll make a note in my official report that he refused your advice,' I said.

Brian sat up straight. 'You'd do that for me?'

'Of course,' I said. 'We're in the same line of business, aren't we? Now, how much did you know about Sir Dennis, before you got the job as his bodyguard?'

Brian shrugged. 'Saw him on the news a few times . . . I know he was involved in some sort of scandal, but I couldn't tell you what it was about; there's been so many recently. If it were up to me, I'd shoot the lot of them and start over. Though that's probably not the best thing to be saying right now . . . I remember him talking to reporters outside his big house, with the dutiful wife hanging on his arm. He was denying everything, and she was saying how she'd stand by him. He was trying to sound innocent but missing by a mile; and she looked like she wanted to ram a grenade up his arse and then show him the pin.' Brian frowned. 'What was the scandal about? Could it be connected to what's happened?'

'If it was important enough to justify hiring a professional assassin, I think I would have been told,' I said carefully. 'Did you ever get the feeling that Sir Dennis might have been keeping something from you?'

'He was a politician,' said Brian.

I nodded, acknowledging the point, and then sat back and looked at him thoughtfully. I let him sweat for a moment, to see if the pressure would bring anything else to the surface. But Brian just stared coldly back at me. He was quite capable of taking the strain. All I could see in his face was a clear determination not to take the blame for anything. Which was, of course, why he was so ready for me to take over the investigation. And yet . . . I couldn't help wondering why he hadn't found some way to stand guard outside the toilet. Sir Dennis might have ordered him not to, but Brian had a much better idea of the risks involved. He could have sneaked down the aisle and stood guard until Sir Dennis finished his business, and then rushed back to his seat again. If he timed it right, Sir Dennis would never have known his orders had been flouted.

And even if Sir Dennis had found out, what could he have done about it? It wasn't as if he could fire his own bodyguard. He was stuck with Brian all the way to Bath. At worst, he might have turned in a scathing report, but that would have been water off a duck's back to an old soldier like Brian.

'What are you thinking about, Jones?' said Brian.

'Just deciding what questions I'm going to ask the others,' I said.

He sniffed loudly. 'You're welcome to them. I'm not used to dealing with civilians. You always know where you are in the military. It's always going to be about rank and orders and duty. Clear cut, every time. Finding out what people are getting up to, and then putting a stop to it. You really think you can get those three to open up to you? We'll be at Bath in less than an hour.'

'One of them must know something,' I said.

'But none of them left this compartment at any point,' Brian said stubbornly. 'I would have seen them.'

'Are you sure you didn't turn your gaze away, just for a moment?' I said. 'Maybe to glance out of the window?'

'It's dark,' said Brian. 'What's there to look at?'

'Rupert Hall went to the toilet,' I said thoughtfully. 'About ten minutes before Sir Dennis.'

Brian looked at me sharply. 'You think he might have been setting up something?'

'It's possible.'

'Like what?'

'I don't know,' I said. It seemed to me I was saying that a lot. 'But if I didn't see anything suspicious, and neither did you or Penny, that can only mean we must all have missed something.'

'Such as?'

'If I knew that,' I said, 'I wouldn't need to question everyone, would I?'

'Right,' said Brian. He frowned again, thinking hard and making heavy going of it. 'The next carriage along is empty, locked off and guarded . . . We got lucky there. Otherwise, you'd have to question everyone on the train. You really think this was a professional hit?'

'I couldn't find any trace of a struggle,' I said. 'And even allowing for the fact that Sir Dennis must have been caught quite literally with his pants down, he should still have had time to react. To put up some kind of a fight.'

'Unless he froze,' said Brian. 'That happens more often than you'd think, the first time people come face to face with a real threat.'

'Even when their life is in danger?'

'Especially then,' said Brian. 'Someone actually trying to kill you is so far out of most people's experience that they have no idea how to handle it. You have to be taught how to react properly. Of course, there's always the chance Sir Dennis knew his killer, and for some reason didn't see them as a threat until it was too late.'

'I thought that,' I said.

It took a moment before what I was saying sank in, and then Brian sat forward in his seat and glared at me.

'The only person he knew on this train was me! And your

partner can confirm that I never left my seat till you came back and announced that Sir Dennis was dead!'

'I could say the same thing about the three business types,' I said reasonably. 'And it wouldn't be difficult for a trained soldier like you to break a man's neck with one blow.'

'What possible reason could I have to kill Sir Dennis?'

'Because he was an arrogant little creep?'

Brian stared at me for a long moment.

'So I'm a suspect?' he said finally.

'Everyone in this carriage has to be a suspect,' I said. 'Apart from Penny and me, of course.'

'Who vouches for you?' said Brian.

'I do,' I said.

Brian sat back in his seat. He thought hard, turning everything over in his mind, and then looked at me for a long moment, as though trying to decide whether or not he could trust me with something.

'Unless he literally never saw his killer coming,' he said finally. 'I know about the Psychic Weapons Division. I couldn't resist taking a quick look at Sir Dennis's file while he was away! Just to see what was so important . . . and as a small act of defiance, for the way he'd been treating me. But once I saw the title page, that was enough for me. I don't know anything about psychic weapons, and I don't want to. I like being able to sleep at night. That's why I put the file up there in the luggage rack – so I wouldn't be tempted to look at it again. But now . . . I'm guessing you know all about that stuff. If there is a professional psychic killer on this train, could they make themselves invisible? Could that be why Sir Dennis didn't react – because all he saw was the toilet door opening on its own?'

'It's possible,' I said.

'I was really hoping you weren't going to say that.' Brian looked at me unhappily. 'What if while we're looking for the killer, he's hiding behind an invisibility cloak and reading our minds? He could know all our plans, all our secrets . . .'

His voice was becoming uncomfortably loud as he struggled to cope with ideas way outside his experience.

'Take it easy,' I said. 'He can't be that good, because he didn't know about Penny and me.'

'But what if he did!' Brian shot back. 'What if he's known about you all along, and he's so good he just doesn't care?'

'No one's that good,' I said flatly. 'Calm down, Brian. I don't believe there's an invisible psychic hiding on this train, and neither should you. It's much more likely that what we're dealing with is just a really clever professional. Now . . . I need you to go and guard the door between here and the vestibule. No one is to enter or leave this compartment without my permission.'

Brian nodded quickly. He felt better now he'd been given orders and something to do.

'Can I have my gun back?'

'You're a big man,' I said. 'Just fill the doorway and give anyone a good glare if they get too close.'

'What if the killer has a gun?'

'Improvise.'

I rose to my feet, stepped out into the aisle and looked steadily at Brian until he heaved a long-suffering sigh and got to his feet.

'You'd make a great officer,' he said.

'Somehow, I don't think that's a compliment,' I said.

'Got that right,' said Brian. 'Tell me: did Sir Dennis really die sitting on the toilet, with his trousers round his ankles?'

I nodded, and Brian laughed briefly.

'Good. Serves him right.'

He marched down the aisle to the end door, about-turned with military precision and set his back against it. He then scowled fiercely down the compartment, to dissuade anyone from even thinking of trying something. I nodded to him, to show I appreciated the effort, and then made my way back to the three businesspeople, hoping they'd be in more of a mood to talk to me, now that Penny had had some time to soften them up a little. I needed something I could use.

It was possible that Brian was the killer. No one had more opportunity than him. Could he have somehow fixed the draw, as a way to get close to Sir Dennis? But in the end Sir Dennis only died when he became temporarily separated from his bodyguard, through his own bad judgement. And, of

course, Brian had never left his seat. Like everyone else in
the compartment.

I had a growing suspicion this was going to be one of those
cases where I suddenly stopped and slapped myself on the
forehead and said, *Of course! How could I have missed that?
It's so obvious!* But that didn't help now. Hindsight can be
very irritating, not to mention unbearably smug.

I found Penny chatting cheerfully with the three businesspeople, who were all looking a lot more relaxed. I cleared my
throat politely, and they broke off immediately, looking at me
with faces that were trying really hard not to give anything
away. Not necessarily because they were guilty, but simply
because they had no reason to trust me. I gestured for Penny
to come and join me, and we moved off down the aisle.

'Have they told you anything useful yet?' I said quietly.
'Hell, I'm ready to settle for something interesting.'

'I haven't found out much,' said Penny. 'The murder has
left them in such a state; it's all they can talk about. Every
time I try to get one of them to open up to me, one of the
others will insist on dragging the conversation back to Sir
Dennis and the horrible way he died.'

'I'll have to question them separately,' I said. 'And I
think I'm going to have to do that without you.'

Penny raised an eyebrow. 'Are you saying you don't
think I can handle a simple interrogation?'

'I just think these people might be more willing to open
up to me about private matters if there wasn't a witness,' I
said carefully. 'And there is always the chance I might have
to get a little harsh, to persuade them to tell me things they
don't want to talk about. If that doesn't work, I can give you
the nod, and you can come rushing in to rescue them from
me. Bad cop, good cop; you know how it works.'

'You can forget that right now,' Penny said flatly. 'You won't
get anything out of these people without my help. All three
of them are halfway into shock; if you try to pressure them,
they'll just clam up.'

I shrugged. 'All right, you take the lead. I'll just sit back
and listen, and butt in if I spot something. Interrogation has
never been what I do best.'

'Or me,' said Penny. 'But it's all we've got.'

'Along with a deadline,' I said.

'How much time do we have?'

'Best not to think about it.'

'You're the one who brought it up!' said Penny.

'And I really wish I hadn't.'

We went back to the three businesspeople, and they all gave me the same suspicious look. They could tell I wasn't on their side. I studied each face carefully. I could see fear and worry, but nothing that looked like guilt. Unfortunately, with every minute that passed, the train was getting closer to Bath – and the point where I'd have no choice but to just give up and let everybody go. So all Penny and I could do was go charging in like a bull in a china shop, and keep hitting people with questions until someone told us something we could use.

I realized I'd been standing there staring at the businesspeople for some time, saying nothing. And probably frowning. I quickly switched to my best apologetic smile, but they just stared coldly back at me, not giving an inch. So I gave up on the smile, started talking and hoped for the best.

'Penny and I were put on this train because there'd been advance warning of a threat against Sir Dennis. Our superiors had no clear information as to what this threat might be, so we were just told to keep our eyes open. That didn't work out too well. Now it's vital we find the killer before we arrive in Bath.'

'Why would anyone want to kill Sir Dennis?' Sita said bullishly. 'He wasn't anyone important. Just a career arsehole.'

'We're assuming it's something to do with his new promotion,' I said. 'Or, failing that, something to do with his private life. Either way, Penny and I are going to have to ask all of you a few questions, if only to eliminate you from our enquiries.'

I looked around, but no one nodded agreement or even tried to argue the point. They just sat stiffly in their seats, staring resentfully back at me. I gave Penny the nod, and she stepped forward, giving them her best *Let's all be friends, you can trust me* smile.

'OK! Let's start with why you all happened to choose this particular train, on this particular evening.'

They all looked at each other, hoping someone else would start the ball rolling. In the end, Rupert Hall cracked first, because he didn't have the nerve to stay silent with both Penny and me staring at him.

'I took this train because it was an express,' he said quietly. 'The quickest way to get to Bath. I'm meeting someone important.'

I waited, but that was all he was prepared to say. And he had to keep his eyes on the floor just to get those few words out. I found it interesting that he still didn't want to say whom he was meeting, or why it was so important that he had to get there in a hurry.

Howard Goldwasser cleared his throat uncomfortably as Penny fixed him with her most engaging smile. He had no trouble looking at Penny or me, but his whole bearing made it clear he was only prepared to say so much and no more.

'It's just a business trip,' he said flatly. 'And this was the first train getting ready to leave when I arrived at the station.'

Once again, what he didn't say was more interesting than what he did. He hadn't explained what kind of business he was in, or the point of his trip, or whether he was planning to meet anyone.

I turned to Sita Patel, but she just sat there and glowered at me and Penny, defying us to get one word out of her. Which was extremely interesting. What could she possibly have to hide that was so important she wasn't even prepared to cooperate in a murder investigation? No matter how guilty it made her look.

'All right,' I said. 'We'll just have to do this the hard way. Penny and I will talk to each of you separately.'

'Why can't this wait till we get to Bath?' Sita said immediately, unable to keep quiet now she'd spotted an opening. 'I mean, aren't we entitled to lawyers if you're going to question us about our possible involvement in a murder?'

'Do you think you're going to need a lawyer?' I said.

'How can I tell, until I know what kind of questions you're going to ask?' Sita shot straight back at me.

'You might want to consider this,' said Penny. 'It's always

possible that the murderer, whoever that turns out to be, might decide they need to do away with all of us before we get to Bath, rather than leave any potential witnesses.'

'But we didn't see anything!' said Rupert. He wriggled uncomfortably in his seat, not wanting to be the centre of attention but unable to stay quiet. 'We didn't even know this politician was dead until Mr Jones told us!'

'We have reason to believe Sir Dennis's killer has to be someone in this compartment,' I said carefully.

Sita jumped on that one straight away. 'What reason?'

'The next carriage along is locked off,' I said. 'So no one from the other end of the train could have got to Sir Dennis.'

They all looked round sharply, seeing each other in a whole new light and really not liking what they saw. I think they would have edged away from each other if they hadn't been trapped in their seats.

'Since I have no idea how the killer could have got to Sir Dennis, any one of you might have noticed something significant,' I said, after I'd given them a while to think about it. 'There's always the chance you saw or heard something that the killer can't allow you to tell someone else.'

They really didn't like the sound of that.

'What if . . . we don't feel like answering some of your questions?' said Rupert. He'd finally found the strength to meet my gaze and was trying hard to sound defiant, but mostly he just came across as troubled. 'What if we decide they're too . . . personal?'

I looked at him thoughtfully. He wasn't the one I would have expected to slam on the brakes this early in the proceedings.

'Not answering isn't going to be an option,' I said.

Something in the way I said that, or something in my gaze, made both Rupert and Howard look away. While Sita just glared at me even harder. And I realized that while I might have established my authority, I'd just thrown away any sympathy the three of them might have had for my position. I never was any good at this interrogation thing. I looked at Penny to rescue me.

'We'll carry out our questioning in as civilized a manner as possible,' she said soothingly. 'We're only interested in identifying the killer. Not your personal lives or backgrounds.'

'Unless they turn out to be connected to the killing,' I said.

'So it's going to be good cop, bad cop, is it?' said Howard. 'Don't look so surprised. I watch television. I know how this works.' He looked at me steadily, almost indifferently. 'Just ask your questions, so we can get this over with.'

'All right,' I said. 'The first order of business is to confiscate all your phones and laptops.' I raised a hand to forestall their immediate objections. 'They'll be put somewhere safe and returned to you later. But for now we can't allow any communications with the outside world.'

'Why not?' said Sita. She sounded outraged at the very thought of being cut off from everyone.

'We can't risk the killer talking to his people,' I said. 'Either to confirm Sir Dennis's death or to ask for assistance. And it's important that the world doesn't know what's happened, just yet. For security reasons.'

The three businesspeople looked sullenly back at me. It seemed the magic word *security* was losing some of its power.

'You have no right to do this!' Sita said loudly. 'You just want to keep us isolated, and frightened, and helpless . . . so you'll have an easier time intimidating us!'

'I told you, I'm meeting someone,' said Rupert. 'I need to be able to contact them if it looks like I'm going to be late.'

'I have a room booked at a hotel in Bath,' said Howard. 'I don't want them giving it to someone else.'

'What's in my phone and on my laptop is my business,' Sita said flatly. 'I'm not having you looking at them.' She looked fiercely at the others. 'I told you this would happen. Told you we couldn't trust them. Don't give in! He can't take our property away from us if we won't let him.'

'We'll be in Bath in under an hour,' I said to Rupert and Howard. 'Your lives won't grind to a halt just because you're going to be out of touch for a while.' I turned to Sita. 'And unless you've been looking up Assassins R Us, I don't give a damn about your browser history.'

'It's just routine procedure,' Penny said soothingly. 'No reason for any of you to take this personally.'

I looked down the aisle at Brian. 'I'm going to need your phone as well.'

He looked back at me, lost for words, openly affronted at being lumped in with the other suspects.

'I need you to set a good example, Brian,' I said.

He nodded stiffly, strode down the aisle, took out his phone and thrust it at me. I accepted it, and Brian glared meaningfully at the other passengers before stomping back down the aisle to take up his position at the door again.

The businesspeople looked at each other, and Rupert and Howard finally nodded grudgingly. Penny and I stood back, so the three of them could get up and go back to their seats. They gathered up their phones and laptops, and Rupert and Howard handed theirs over to Penny without a word. Sita handed over her phone, but clutched her laptop tightly to her chest, defying me to wrestle it away from her. I was pretty sure I could, but I was curious. What could she possibly have on there that she was so determined to keep from me? Well, when in doubt, be direct.

'What's so important about your laptop, Sita?' I said bluntly. 'And just what have you been working at so busily all this time?'

Sita scowled at me, started to say something and then broke off, as she realized Rupert and Howard were looking at her suspiciously, wondering what it was she was trying so hard to hide.

'All right!' she said. 'If you must know . . . I'm a journalist. I work for the *Evening Standard*, covering the political beat. I got on this train because I was following a story, over Sir Dennis's sudden and very unexpected promotion to a top-level job.'

Rupert and Howard looked at her disappointedly. She wasn't one of them after all. Sita didn't notice because she was too busy trying to stare me down.

'What kind of story were you pursuing?' I said.

'Nothing worth Sir Dennis getting killed over,' said Sita. 'Just mutterings about him getting a job he really wasn't entitled to. Sir Dennis has always been a bit dodgy, but this looked as if it might have the makings of a major scandal. So

I booked a seat here in First Class in the hope I'd get an opportunity to back Sir Dennis into a corner, and hit him with some really awkward questions. I was still trying to figure out how to get him on his own, away from his bodyguard, when suddenly he was dead. But that just makes this story even more important! I'm not giving up all my notes and background quotes, and clues as to who my sources are!'

'You don't have to,' I said patiently. 'I'm not interested in spiking your story; I just need you to postpone sending it in.'

I noticed that Rupert and Howard were starting to look a little uncertain now, and wondering whether they could get away with demanding their laptops back.

'All right!' I said. 'How about this? If you give up your laptops voluntarily, you'll all get them back when we arrive in Bath. If I have to take them from you by force – and I will if I have to – I'll have no choice but to hand them over to our computer experts. And they'll look at everything. You really want to go that route?'

'Bully,' said Sita.

But the strength had gone out of her. She thrust her laptop at me, and I handed it over to Penny, who had to struggle to avoid dropping everything. I nodded to the luggage rack, where Brian had put Sir Dennis's file, and Penny glared at me before rising up on tiptoe to dump the phones and laptops in the rack. In clear sight of everyone, but well out of easy reach.

'Any more indignities you want to put us through?' said Sita.

'I'm afraid so,' I said. 'Before we go any further, I need to check all of you for weapons.'

'I am not being frisked,' said Sita ominously.

'You told us Sir Dennis died from a broken neck,' said Howard. 'You don't need a weapon for that.'

'Our advance intelligence was pretty sure the killer would be a professional,' I said. 'So I need to make sure that you're not armed.' I looked to Sita. 'Penny can check you out.'

'I am not being frisked!' Sita repeated loudly.

'It'll be just like airport security,' said Penny.

'I could always ask Brian to do it,' I said.

'Love to,' said Brian from the door.

'In your dreams,' snapped Sita.

In the end, she went along with it. No one really objected, if only because they all wanted to be sure no one else had a weapon. Penny and I were brisk and efficient, and turned up nothing. Which was no more than I'd expected. I only did it because I would have felt such an idiot if I didn't do it and the killer suddenly produced a gun at an inconvenient moment.

'Hey, Jones!' Brian said suddenly. I looked round to see him step away from the door as Dee the refreshments lady entered the compartment, pushing her trolley ahead of her. She had to put some effort into it; the squeaking wheels were really giving her trouble now, apparently determined to go shooting off in every direction at once. Dee wrestled the trolley into submission and then stopped as Brian grabbed her by the arm. She looked at him in surprise, while he looked down the aisle at me.

'Should I let her in?'

'Technically speaking, I would have to say you've left it a bit late to ask,' I said. 'I thought I made it clear to you that no one was to be allowed into this compartment without my permission.'

'I thought you might want to question her,' said Brian, entirely unmoved by the disapproval in my voice. 'She was in here not long before Sir Dennis was killed, remember? And since you're the one who made such a fuss over being the man in charge, Mr Jones, you get to make the decisions.'

I think, in the army, the look on his face would have been enough for a charge of dumb insolence. But he did have a point. Dee had been here, so she might have seen or heard something. I nodded to Brian and he let go of Dee's arm. She looked at him and then at me, before finally setting off again. The squeaking of the trolley wheels was very loud in the sudden quiet. Dee looked around her uncertainly, picking up on the tense atmosphere and clearly wondering what she was walking into. I went forward to meet her.

'It's only me, darling,' she said brightly. 'With my little trolley, here to help you out!'

'Didn't the guard tell you this compartment is off limits to everyone until we get to Bath?' I said sternly.

'Eric told me what happened to Sir Dennis,' Dee said quickly. 'About his being dead and everything. So I thought you people might need some looking after. Hot sweet tea is very good for shock. Everybody knows that.'

'Eric wasn't supposed to tell any of the train staff about Sir Dennis.'

'Oh, he hasn't told anyone else, darling,' said Dee. 'He's been very good. He only told me because I sort of made him. When he came back down the train, he was in such a state that I thought I'd better sit him down and find out what was wrong. So I gave him a hug and a shoulder to cry on, and once he started talking, he couldn't stop, the poor dear. He told me all about Sir Dennis, and you, and . . . well, everything! He's feeling a lot better now. In case you were wondering.'

'I gave Eric strict orders that the far door to the next carriage was to remain locked,' I said sternly.

'I had Eric open it up, just for me,' said Dee, entirely unbothered by my tone. 'So I could bring my trolley through. Trust me, you'll all feel a lot better for having a nice hot drink inside you, to calm your nerves and settle you down.'

I started to say something, but Dee just kept going and talked right over me. And I let her, because I was fascinated to hear what she'd say next.

'You don't need to worry; Eric locked the door behind me, to make sure no one else could come through. Though I can't see why anyone would want to. That whole carriage is dark as anything. I had to feel my way down the aisle, with the trolley fighting me every step of the way. I've got bruises everywhere. Eric's still trying to get the lights back on, but I think he's a bit out of his depth, to be honest.'

She paused to get her breath, and I jumped in while I had the chance.

'Are you and Eric close? Away from the train, I mean?'

'Oh, no,' she said quickly. 'Hardly know the man. This is my first day on the job. You can tell, can't you? It's really not what I was expecting . . .' She looked at me uncertainly. 'Have I done something wrong? Should I go?'

I was about to say yes, when simple curiosity got the better of me. Dee must have worked really hard on Eric to get him to open the carriage door after I told him not to, which suggested Dee must have a really good reason for wanting to be here. And I wanted to know what that was.

'Go ahead, Dee,' I said. 'See if anyone wants anything.'

She smiled quickly and threw her whole weight against the trolley to get it moving again. She manoeuvred the awkward thing down the aisle, offering hot drinks and all manner of snacks, but this time there were no takers. They were all just waiting for her to leave, so they could go back to talking about the only thing that mattered: the murder, and how it affected them. So they all just shook their heads or looked away, until Dee got to Rupert Hall. And just as before, Dee focused in on him. She crouched down beside his seat, smiling warmly.

'What's the matter, darling? You don't look at all well. Why not eat something?'

She kept trying to tempt him with one brightly packaged treat after another, almost forcing them into his hands, but he wouldn't even look at them. He just kept saying he didn't want anything, and Dee just kept ignoring him. Penny shot me a look, clearly wondering why I wasn't intervening. I nodded for her to move in closer and keep an eye on Dee. I was wondering where all of this was going. Eventually, Dee gave up, put everything back on her trolley and then casually picked up something hidden among the plastic teacups. And that was when Penny shot out a hand and grabbed hold of Dee's wrist. Dee tried to wrench her arm away, but Penny had her pinned firmly in place.

Dee's face became suddenly cold and set, her friendly chatty persona gone in a moment. Penny twisted Dee's wrist hard, and something dropped out of Dee's hand on to the floor. I stepped in quickly and picked up a small spy camera.

Dee wrenched her arm out of Penny's grasp, darted round the trolley and made a run for the door, only to come face to face with Brian, blocking the way with his body. He smiled at her, and it was a really unpleasant smile. And I finally understood why he'd let her through. He'd found her presence suspicious, so he let her in to give her enough rope to hang herself with. Brian looked very pleased at seeing his suspicions confirmed and having someone he could take out his frustrations on. Dee headed straight for him anyway.

Brian reached out to grab hold of her, and Dee kicked him hard in the right knee. Brian cried out, in shock and surprise as much as pain. His leg collapsed under him and he lurched to one side, away from the door. Dee threw herself forward and the door hissed open, but by then I'd caught up with her.

I grabbed Dee by the shoulder and hauled her back into the carriage. She fought me all the way but couldn't break my grip. So she twisted around inside it, grabbed hold of the front of my jacket and tried for a classic judo throw. But I just braced myself and refused to be thrown. Dee immediately released her hold and fell back a step. Her face was perfectly calm and composed, like any professional at work. She struck out at me, unleashing a series of powerful kicks and blows, but I dodged them all easily. My reflexes are so much faster than human that any fight is always going to seem to me as if it's in slow motion. Dee broke off her attacks the moment it became clear she wasn't getting anywhere. She was breathing hard. I wasn't. Dee dropped her hands, straightened up and shrugged resignedly.

'Just my luck, to run into someone who knows how to fight. OK, I surrender, all right? What are you going to do? Confiscate my trolley?'

Sita suddenly jumped to her feet and stabbed an accusing finger at Dee. 'She's a professional fighter! We all saw it! She must be the killer!'

'What?' said Dee. She looked startled for the first time, caught completely off balance by the accusation. 'Of course I'm not the killer!'

Brian hurried down the aisle, favouring his aching knee, and grabbed hold of Dee's shoulder from behind. His hand clamped down so hard it made Dee wince despite herself, but she didn't cry out or try to pull away. She kept her gaze fixed on me, because she knew I was the one she had to convince.

'Who are you? Who are you working for?' Brian shouted right into her face.

'My name is Dee Calder,' she said steadily. 'I work for the Super Sunshine Detective Agency, based in London. I'm a private detective.'

'Yeah, right,' said Brian. His voice was thick with anger, embarrassed at being taken down so easily.

'That's enough,' I said to Brian. 'Let her go.'

Brian suddenly seemed to realize that he was intimidating a middle-aged woman. He snatched his hand away from her shoulder and stepped back. Dee nodded briefly to me in thanks, her face perfectly composed, as though nothing unpleasant had happened.

'Why are you here, Dee?' I said. 'Really?'

She started to reach inside her jacket pocket and then stopped as I fixed her with a warning look.

'Whatever that is,' I said. 'I think you'd better take it out slowly and carefully, thumb and forefinger only.'

'Glad to see there's another professional on this train,' said Dee. 'Don't worry, darling; it's only my ID.'

She produced a laminated card and held it out for me to read. I let her hold it while I studied the details. The card confirmed she was who she said she was, and that she did indeed work for the improbably named detective agency.

'Looks like the real deal,' I said finally. 'You can put it away now.'

'Oh, come on!' said Brian, unable to contain himself. 'Anyone can fake an ID!'

'Let's face it, Brian,' said Penny, moving in beside me. 'She doesn't exactly look like a professional assassin, does she?'

'They never do,' Brian said darkly. 'That's the point.'

'Arrested many assassins, have you?' I said.

'Don't make fun of me,' said Brian. His voice was flat, and his hands had clenched into fists at his sides.

'Wouldn't dream of it,' I said. I turned back to Dee. 'So, what's a private detective doing on this train? And why make such an effort to get in here, only to ignore what happened to the dead VIP?'

'I don't give a damn about Sir Dennis,' said Dee. 'I'm here for him.'

And she pointed at Rupert Hall, who couldn't have been more astonished if she'd aimed a gun at him.

'Me?' he said, his voice rising sharply. 'Why me?'

'Yes,' said Penny. 'What's so special about him?' And then she stopped and looked apologetically at Rupert. 'No offence.'

'That's all right,' said Rupert. 'I was wondering the same thing myself.'

'Why are we listening to this woman?' Brian said loudly. 'She's only trying to distract us . . .'

'Brian,' I said sharply, and his gaze snapped back to me. 'Go back and guard the door, please. If she could get through the darkened carriage, there's always the chance someone else might show up.'

Brian nodded reluctantly, shot Dee a final angry look and limped back down the aisle with as much dignity as he could manage. Dee allowed herself to relax a little once he was safely out of range.

'I'm working for Rupert Hall's wife,' she said steadily. 'Because she thinks he's cheating on her. That he's only going to Bath this evening so he can meet up with his girlfriend. I was put on this train to gather evidence.'

All the colour had dropped out of Rupert's face. He started to say something but couldn't get the words out. And then he suddenly leaned forward and buried his face in his hands.

'See?' said Dee. 'Told you. The agency got me this job as tea lady, and told me to get his fingerprints on some packaging, or, failing that, some photos.'

'And if you couldn't?' I said.

Dee shrugged. 'Someone else will be waiting in Bath, to follow him wherever he goes and identify whoever it is he's meeting.'

I looked at her thoughtfully. 'That seems like a lot of trouble to go to, for a simple adultery case.'

'I said that,' said Dee. 'But apparently the wife is rich. And I mean big-time loaded. And very determined that if this does end up in the divorce courts, lover boy there isn't going to be in a position to walk away with any of it.'

'But you knew a man had been murdered back here,' Penny said suddenly. 'Why were you so determined to enter a crime scene, just to have another go at Rupert?'

'Because this was my last chance to get some hard evidence on him, before we get to Bath,' said Dee.

'Was that your only reason?' said Penny.

Dee smiled briefly. 'No hard evidence, no bonus.'

'I'm confiscating your camera,' I said. Because I couldn't be sure she hadn't taken some photos earlier that might have included me. 'Leave Mr Hall alone now, please. Go back down the train to where you came from and stay well away from this carriage. And take your noisy trolley with you.'

Dee nodded quickly, got behind her trolley and headed for the door. Brian watched her approaching but made no move to get out of her way.

'Play nicely now, Brian,' I said warningly. 'Don't make me have to come over there.'

Dee pushed her trolley straight at Brian, in a way that suggested she was perfectly ready to drive it through and, if need be, right over him.

'You heard the man,' she said.

Brian moved to one side at the very last moment, still favouring his injured knee. Dee pushed her trolley past Brian and managed to steer at least three of the trolley's wheels over both of his feet. He stared straight ahead, refusing to admit anything was happening. I waited till Dee had entered the vestibule and then called out her name. She stopped abruptly and looked back. I took my time walking down the aisle and finally joined her in the vestibule so I could talk to her quietly.

'Don't speak to anyone about what's happened here,' I said. 'Or I will talk to the right people and have your licence lifted. And once you've passed through the darkened carriage, tell Eric he is to lock the far door, keep it locked and guard it. I don't want to see anyone else coming this way, for any reason.'

'Have I dropped Eric in it?' said Dee. 'He wouldn't have talked about any of this if I hadn't persuaded him.'

'He's not in any trouble,' I said. 'As long as you leave him alone.'

Dee nodded quickly and headed for the next carriage as fast her trolley would allow. I watched her disappear into the darkness and then listened until the squeaking wheels passed through the far door. I went back into First Class. Brian immediately took up his position guarding the door again, flexing his aching knee and glaring at me as if it was all my fault.

I went back down the aisle to talk to Rupert Hall. He no longer had his head in his hands, but he was still bent right over in his seat and looked as if he might fall apart at any moment. Penny was hovering over him, but he wouldn't even look at her. She shot me a stern look and then stepped back out of the way. I stood over Rupert and said his name. He slowly raised his head. He hadn't been crying but he looked as if he wanted to. His eyes seemed bruised, as though life had just taken a hard swing at him.

'I'm really not interested in your domestic problems, Rupert,' I said. 'Though I may have to ask you a few questions about them, just to make sure they're not connected to Sir Dennis's death. You take it easy for a while, and I'll get back to you when you're feeling stronger.'

He had to swallow hard before he could say anything, and even then his voice was little more than a whisper.

'Thank you. I could use a little time to myself. Before I have to talk about things I never wanted to talk about.'

I turned to look at Howard Goldwasser, on the other side of the aisle. To give the man credit, he'd been staring out of the window and doing his best not to listen to what Rupert and I were saying. I said his name, and he immediately turned to face me. He met my gaze unflinchingly, making it very clear he didn't give a damn what I wanted to ask him. I had no idea what that was about, but I was determined to find out.

'I have to start with someone,' I said. 'Are you ready to answer a few questions, Howard?'

'Go ahead,' he said flatly. 'Ask me anything. It won't do you any good. I don't know anything you want to know.'

Sita started to object on Howard's behalf, half rising out of her seat, but he just glanced at her and shook his head. She slumped reluctantly back into her seat, scowling heavily as though he'd let her down.

'Take a short walk with me, Howard,' I said. 'Just a comfortable distance away from everyone else, so we can have some privacy while we talk.'

He shrugged and took his time getting to his feet. Not to make any point, as far as I could tell, but because he genuinely didn't care about any of this. I waited patiently for him to join me in the aisle, and then Penny and I escorted him to a seat further down the carriage. I sat opposite Howard, studying him thoughtfully. Penny shot him a quick reassuring smile as she settled down beside me.

Howard looked at both of us with equal indifference. There was nothing in his face to suggest he felt at all threatened, by us or the general situation. Which was interesting. I looked to Penny to start things off, and she plunged right in as though she had every confidence in what she was doing. She smiled brightly at Howard and addressed him in an open, friendly tone, as though we were just chatting.

'Let's start with the easy stuff, Howard. You said you were on a business trip. What kind of business are you in?'

'Office supplies, with contracts to the MOD,' he said. 'You'd be surprised how much paperwork they still get through every day. The MOD has been very slow to embrace computers. Except for when it comes to weapons, of course.'

He stared impassively at Penny and me. His voice had been almost defiantly indifferent. As though none of this mattered.

'How did you know Sir Dennis?' said Penny.

'What makes you think I did?'

'I saw you look at him,' I said patiently. 'In a way that made it clear you knew who he was. And that you weren't too keen on him.'

Howard shrugged, not bothered in the least at having been caught out in an evasion so early in the proceedings.

'All right, I knew the man. Never met him before, never wanted to. But I had good reason to know who he was. I'm no longer with the firm I used to work for, because a few years back Sir Dennis suddenly decided to change all the rules, completely rewriting the conditions under which competing firms could bid for tenders. Not to encourage efficiency, or even to follow up on a political promise. He just did it to support those firms he had a financial stake in. The bastard.

'He made a fortune, while firms like the one I used to work for went to the wall. It all came out later, of course. There was a medium-sized scandal, but it wasn't sexy enough to hold the public's attention for long. So there was just a lot of finger-wagging and name-calling in Parliament, and in the end Sir Dennis walked away without a stain on his portfolio. Because he had connections. While my old firm lost a lot of its contracts and had to lay off a lot of people. Including me.'

'So you had good reason to hate Sir Dennis,' said Penny.

Howard shook his head firmly. 'No. In his own back-handed way, he did me a good turn. Because when I started with my new firm, I met the woman who became my second wife. The job is secure, I'm making good money, and I've never been happier. And all because Sir Dennis couldn't keep his snout out of the trough.'

'Who are you working for now?' I said.

'Same line of business. It's what I know.'

'Why are you going to Bath?' said Penny.

'Business convention,' said Howard. 'The usual thing: check out the new lines and decide which ones are worth recommending to my bosses. Not very glamorous, I suppose, but it all helps to keep the wheels turning.'

I nodded. Howard was being very concise and to the point, never once hesitating in his answers. But that isn't how most people talk. It sounded as if he'd spent some time carefully rehearsing what he was going to say to us, to make sure it would sound convincing. So Penny and I would go away and leave him alone. Most of all, his face didn't match what he was saying. There was no interest in his voice when he talked about his job, and he hadn't even mentioned the name of the new love in his life.

And on top of all that, there was nothing in his gaze as he looked at me or Penny, not necessarily because he was trying to hide something, but more as though he simply couldn't be bothered. Because he had something more important on his mind.

I looked at Penny, and she looked at me for a cue on how to proceed. We'd asked all the obvious questions and received a set of perfectly acceptable answers. I wasn't sure I believed any of them, but I didn't feel like pressing him. For the moment. Better to let him go back to his seat and think he'd put one over on us. I nodded to Penny.

'Thank you, Howard,' said Penny. 'That's enough for now.'

'One last question,' I said. 'What was it you were working on earlier, on your laptop?'

And Howard froze. He looked at me and then at Penny, but he didn't say anything. He hadn't expected that question and he didn't have a prepared answer. He licked his lips, forced out a smile and got ready to lie.

'Just a few notes. For a report I have to write. The one part of the job I hate. I've never been any good at that sort of thing.'

I waited to see if he might carry on talking and perhaps give something away. But Howard just closed his mouth firmly, as though to keep any more unrehearsed words from spilling out. He made steady eye contact with me for the first time, as though only now taking me seriously as a potential threat. And I couldn't help but wonder: what kind of threat could I possibly pose to him? I smiled easily back at Howard, as though I hadn't noticed anything.

'You can go back to your seat now,' I said. 'Please don't talk to anyone else, until we've finished speaking to them.'

'Of course,' said Howard.

He couldn't get out of his seat fast enough. Rupert and Sita both looked at Howard closely, to see how our questioning had affected him, but he wouldn't even glance at them. He hurried down the aisle, chose a new seat well away from Sita and Rupert, and sat down with his back to Penny and me. I thought he had the air of someone trying to decide whether or not he'd just dodged a bullet. I turned to Penny.

'Well, that was interesting.'

'He was definitely being evasive about something,' said Penny. 'When he told us about finding his wonderful new wife, he didn't smile once. But . . . I'm not sure that whatever he's hiding has anything to do with Sir Dennis. He didn't show any real emotion when he talked about the man. Even when he called him a bastard.'

'Given the way Howard was looking at Sir Dennis earlier, he definitely felt some ill will towards the man,' I said. 'And if Howard is trying to conceal something . . . Why didn't he make more of an effort to convince us he wasn't the killer?'

'I don't think he gives a damn about Sir Dennis being murdered,' said Penny. 'Or anything else, really. It feels to me as though he just wants all of this to be over, because it's getting in the way of whatever else he has on his mind. The only time he showed any interest in what's happening was when he seemed worried he might lose the hotel room he'd booked in Bath.'

'Let him stew for a while,' I said. 'We'll talk to the others and then have another go at him. See if we can crack open a few of these secrets he's so determined to keep hidden from us.'

'I have to say, I think you're doing very well, darling,' said Penny. 'For someone who was so sure he wasn't any good at interrogation.'

'It's not easy,' I said. 'I can't ask our suspects any of the usual questions in a murder case. Like . . . where were you when the victim was killed? We already know the answer. I can't question anyone's alibi for the time of the murder, because we're part of it. All we can do is keep piling the pressure on everyone and hope we can trap someone in an obvious lie . . .'

'Like Howard,' said Penny.

'Exactly,' I said. 'Though I can't help feeling he was merely substituting one lie for another. There's something not right about Howard . . .'

'There's something not right about this whole case,' said Penny.

I smiled. 'We've handled worse. Ready to take a crack at the next suspect?'

'Bring them on,' said Penny. 'Who did you have in mind?'

'I thought Sita Patel.'

'OK,' said Penny. 'This should be fun.'

I stood up and looked down the carriage. Sita met my gaze

immediately, as though she'd expected me to pick her next. She glowered at me challengingly, so I hit her with my most engaging smile.

'Sita,' I said. 'Would you come over and join us, please?'

For a moment, I thought she might actually defy me – as if she wanted me to come and fetch her, and drag her down the aisle by brute force. As though that would prove something. In the end, though, Sita heaved herself up out of her seat and stomped down the aisle, scowling. I couldn't help noticing that Rupert and Howard didn't so much as glance at her, so intent they were on their own thoughts.

Sita dropped into the seat opposite Penny and me, folded her arms tightly and pressed her lips firmly together, to make it clear we weren't getting anything out of her without a struggle. She glared impartially at both of us, as though having trouble deciding who was more deserving of her displeasure. She wanted us to start something, so she could have the satisfaction of fighting her corner. I shot Penny a warning glance, but as usual she was way ahead of me.

'Thanks for helping us out, Sita,' said Penny, smiling encouragingly. 'We'd be grateful for anything you can tell us that might help solve the mystery of what happened to Sir Dennis.'

Sita just stared right back at her, not giving an inch.

'All right, let's start with the basics,' I said, as pleasantly as I could. 'What are you doing on this train, Sita?'

'I told you,' she said flatly. 'I'm a journalist. A staff writer, for the *Evening Standard.*'

'Yes,' Penny said patiently, 'But what story are you working on? What was it in particular about Sir Dennis that caught your attention and brought you here, to this compartment?'

'What's the matter?' said Sita. 'Don't you believe I'm a journalist? Do you want to see my NUJ card?'

'We don't have to be enemies, Sita,' said Penny, in her best *Let's all be reasonable and play nicely* tone.

'Really?' said Sita, raising her chin so she could look down her nose at both of us. 'I'm all about telling people the truth, while your job is to protect the secrets of those in power. All the things people have a right to know. What could we possibly have in common?'

'We all want to find out who killed Sir Dennis, don't we?' I said. 'Wouldn't that make a much bigger story for you to cover?'

Sita looked at me with new interest. 'You'd let me be a part of that?'

'We might,' I said. 'You help us get to the truth about the murder, and we'll see to it you get access to the kind of details that would make for a real exclusive. Of course, if you give us a hard time . . .'

'Oh . . . go on, then; hit me with your questions,' said Sita. 'But I have to be allowed to contact my editor as soon as possible! This is the kind of story that makes careers! You can bet the moment the news gets out that Sir Dennis has been murdered, the rest of the media will be all over this story like fleas on a dog. Right now, I've got the advantage, and I'm damned if I'll give it up.'

'You can have your phone and your laptop back the moment we get to Bath,' said Penny. 'But if you can say you were present when the murderer was captured, that should give you a head start on everyone else. Though, of course, you can't mention Ishmael or me.'

'Like I even know your real names,' said Sita, not bothering to hide a sneer at such obvious pseudonyms.

'Let's try again,' I said. 'What story, exactly, were you pursuing, Sita? What do you know, or think you know, about Sir Dennis and his new appointment?'

'You sound like my editor,' said Sita. 'Always wanting me to be sure of my facts . . .' She sighed deeply and actually relaxed a little as she prepared to tell us the truth at last. 'I got on this train hoping for a chance to pin Sir Dennis to a wall with some really tough questions, in a situation where he wouldn't have his usual protectors to run interference for him. I had to call in some really serious favours to find out which train he was going to be on this evening. But don't ask me who leaked the information because I'll never tell!'

'That's all right,' said Penny. 'We don't need to know.'

Sita looked disappointed, as though she'd been hoping that we would insist on knowing, just so she could tell us to go straight to hell. She probably had a fiery speech already prepared, about the sacred duty of a reporter to protect her sources. She hesitated, and I could see the inner conflict in her eyes. She knew she shouldn't really share any information with the enemy, but she couldn't resist an opportunity to show off to us how much she knew. She leaned forward in her seat, her gaze darting from Penny to me and back again.

'When you're a young reporter just starting out on the political beat in London, and you haven't had a chance to build up your own stable of reliable contacts like the older guys, the best place to pick up useful information is in the bars around Westminster – where the people who work for the people in power go to drink, and try to forget the kind of day they've had. Just by being pleasant and personable, and keeping them company while they drink, and most importantly not bothering them with questions, you can learn a lot.

'Everyone was talking about Sir Dennis being awarded an important new position he definitely wasn't entitled to. I wasn't the only one who found that suspicious. Sir Dennis has never been more than just another arse-kissing functionary. Word is he got his knighthood for warning someone in the last Cabinet that a fetish club they belonged to had been infiltrated by a tabloid journalist.

'Anyway . . . an awful lot of people were spitting feathers over this new promotion, even if none of them seemed to know exactly what it was. Some were outraged because Sir Dennis was getting a job they thought the people they represented should have had, while others were taking it as a personal affront that they hadn't been consulted. They're a fragile lot in politics; they bruise easily.

'I kept my head down and quietly eavesdropped in all directions while they took it in turn to bitch to each other. All I could make out for sure was that Sir Dennis had been appointed head of some really secret part of the MOD. Which was more than usually interesting, because no one with half a brain would let Sir Dennis anywhere near a secret that mattered. So how did he get the job? No one seemed to know – and these were people who prided themselves on knowing the kind of things most people never get to hear about.'

Sita leaned back in her seat, smiling cheerfully. She was on a roll, so involved in impressing us with her insider knowledge that she'd forgotten we were the enemy and not to be trusted.

'I smelled a rat,' she said gleefully. 'A sudden jump that far up the ladder could only be the result of nepotism, cronyism, bribery or blackmail . . . All tactics Sir Dennis had been known to use to get what he wanted but wasn't entitled to.

'Working the political beat taught me to be suspicious of everyone and cynical about everything . . . but Sir Dennis was in a class of his own. An openly corrupt, back-stabbing bottom-feeder, who'd only survived for so long because of all the dirt he could spill if he wasn't kept happy. Not that unusual in today's politics, but the thought of someone like Sir Dennis as head of an MOD department made my blood boil. So I decided to do something about it!'

Sita finally lurched to a halt because she'd run out of steam and had to take a break to get her breath back. She looked searchingly at Penny and me, gauging our reaction to what she'd been telling us. I was perfectly prepared to believe her. I'd heard a lot worse in my time. And Penny took her cue from me. Sita seemed a little taken aback that we weren't more surprised or shocked. I think she would have preferred it if we had been, so she could sneer at our naivety.

'Don't you find it disappointing?' Penny asked Sita. 'Never being able to believe in anyone or anything?'

'Of course not!' said Sita. 'That's what keeps me going! Searching for just the right story I can use to bring one of those arrogant bastards down. When you're fighting power and influence and Very Important Scumbags protecting each other, the truth is the only weapon you have.' And then she stopped and fixed both of us with a sudden scowl. 'Speaking of which, who is it you work for, exactly? Because I'm telling you everything and you're not telling me a damned thing. If I'm going to trust you, I need more than an obvious runaround like *security* to go on.'

'Who do you think we work for?' I said, with just the slightest of smiles.

Sita started to say something and then broke off, as her mind tried to run off in a dozen directions at once. She sat silently, not even looking at Penny or me as she ran through all the possibilities. Or at least the possibilities she knew about. Underground groups survive because no one knows they exist, so if you've even heard of a group, the odds are they're not that important. Several times Sita started to ask me something and then stopped herself. I decided to let her take a break, while I had her off balance. I'd learned a lot from Sita. Not enough to clear or incriminate her, but enough to give me something to think about.

'That's all for now, thank you,' I said.

Sita broke off from her deliberations to look at me sharply. 'Really? I was only just getting started! There's a lot more you need to know, and a hell of a lot more about you two that I need to know!'

'For the moment, we're just getting a feel for who everyone is,' Penny said smoothly. 'We'll get back to you, once we've finished speaking to the others.'

Sita looked at her narrowly and then at me. 'You have to promise to keep me informed.'

'When we know something, you'll know something,' I said.

The look on her face made it clear she wasn't at all convinced about that, but she got up out of her seat with a minimum of bad grace and stalked back down the aisle to her original seat, so she could settle down to some hard thinking. Rupert and Howard both took a break from their deliberations to look at her curiously, probably wondering what she could have been telling Penny and me for so long, but she didn't even glance at them. Penny looked at me expectantly, but all I could do was shrug.

'That was all very interesting,' I said. 'But we're still no closer to figuring out who killed Sir Dennis, or why, or how they did it.'

'At least Sita confirmed what we suspected,' said Penny. 'Sir Dennis wasn't short of enemies. Any number of people had good reason to want him dead. Including people afraid of what a man like Sir Dennis might do once he had access to that kind of power and influence.'

'But I didn't hear anything to suggest that any of these political insiders knew anything about the Psychic Weapons Division,' I said. 'Professional jealousy might result in some parliamentary back-stabbing, but I can't see it as a motive for murder.'

Penny looked at me thoughtfully. 'Do you think Sita knows about the Division?'

'I doubt it. She wouldn't be able to keep a story that big to herself. She'd be hitting us with all kinds of questions, desperate to dig some sort of confirmation out of us. A story about the Division's existence would be much more important than the murder of a mid-level functionary.'

Penny nodded slowly. 'Do you think all that stuff about Sir Dennis was true? Was he really that bad?'

'Wouldn't surprise me,' I said. 'Sita was being very careful to report only what she'd heard from people in a position to know.'

'But there's always the possibility she only told us the things she did in order to avoid telling us something else,' said Penny.

I looked at her. 'Like what?'

Penny smiled ruefully. 'That's the point, isn't it? We were both so fascinated, listening to her spill secrets from behind closed Westminster doors, that we never got a chance to ask her anything about herself. And I can't help thinking that might have been the point.'

I grinned at her. 'You're getting the hang of this interrogation thing. It is frustrating, though, isn't it? Circling round and round the truth, knowing it's there but never being sure whether you're getting any closer.'

'All right, what do we do now?' said Penny.

'Keep asking questions, and checking the answers against each other, until finally something sticks out.'

'And if it doesn't?'

'Then we're in trouble.' I looked down the aisle to where all three passengers were conspicuously not looking at us. 'I think it's time we talked to Rupert.'

'We are not going to browbeat him, Ishmael,' Penny said firmly. 'I think he might actually fall apart under rough handling.'

'Unless that's what we're supposed to think,' I said.

'My brain hurts,' said Penny.

'Join the club,' I said. 'We have T-shirts and secret handshakes.'

I called down the aisle to Rupert. Sita and Howard turned quickly to look at him. Rupert stared at Penny and me for a long moment, not moving. He looked like a man facing the prospect of his own execution. He finally took a deep breath to brace himself, got up from his seat and walked unsteadily down the aisle. His eyes darted back and forth between Penny and me as though trying to decide which of us might prove the most sympathetic. He sat down facing us and folded his hands together in his lap. And perhaps only I would have noticed he was doing that to hide just how much they were shaking.

'It's time to answer a few questions, Rupert,' I said.

'We'll try to get through this as quickly as possible,' Penny said reassuringly. 'How are you feeling, Rupert?'

He shrugged listlessly. His face was drawn and tired, and I only had to look at him to understand he didn't want to say anything because he didn't want to give away something that might be used against him.

'Why are you on this train, Rupert?' said Penny.

'You know why,' he said quietly. 'And I really don't want to talk about it.'

'All right,' I said. 'What kind of business are you in?'

'Import/export,' he said diffidently. 'Bit of this, bit of that. Always looking to find a gap in the market I can take advantage of. Just a snapper-up of unconsidered trifles . . . I used to have that on my business card, but no one ever got it. I never get to deal in anything big or important, but it all adds up to a decent living.' He smiled briefly. 'My wife has never understood why I feel the need to spend so much time running around, chasing down one deal after another. Julia always says she has more than enough money for both of us – and, of course, she does. But I need to be doing something, if only for my pride's sake. And I am very good at it.'

He stopped abruptly, as he realized how much his mouth was running away with him. He'd started out telling us about his business and now he was talking about himself. I watched him make a conscious decision to rein himself in and be more careful about what he was saying. He fixed me with a forced smile, ignoring Penny because she was the sympathetic one. He knew I was the one he had to convince.

'I had never even heard of Sir Dennis before I got on this train,' he said flatly. 'I've never been interested in politicians. Why should I? They're not interested in me.'

'We all heard what Dee had to say,' Penny said gently. 'About why you're going to Bath.'

'Is it true, Rupert?' I said. 'Do you have a girlfriend on the side?'

He winced, as though he'd been hit. 'Please don't put it like that. You make it sound so sordid.'

'It is what it is,' I said. 'Unless you tell us otherwise.'

'Do we have to talk about this?' Rupert said desperately. 'If I give you my word that none of it has anything to do with Sir Dennis?'

'The more you don't want to talk about it, the more we're bound to think we need to know,' Penny said kindly. 'Please, Rupert, just tell us what's going on.'

'You're not the first man to have an affair,' I said. 'What's so special that you have to keep it a secret?'

'Because I don't have a girlfriend,' said Rupert. 'I have a boyfriend.' He broke off to breathe deeply, as though searching for the strength to continue. He looked down at his hands, clasped tightly together in his lap, so he wouldn't have to look at either of us. 'I'm on my way to spend the weekend with him in Bath. We've been seeing each other for almost a year now.' He finally raised his eyes and looked searchingly at both of us, to see how we were taking this. He seemed to find some reassurance in our expressions, and after taking a moment to compose himself, he continued.

'Daniel and I are in love. He has to keep it secret, because of the way his family is, and I keep it quiet because Julia wouldn't understand.' He smiled mirthlessly. 'I'm not sure I do. I still love my wife, I really do. But the time I've spent with Daniel has been the happiest I've ever known.

'You have no idea how much trouble I've gone to, to keep Julia from finding out about Daniel. To keep everyone from finding out . . . that I'm not the kind of man I always thought I was. But I suppose, in the end, I was making so many business trips it was bound to make Julia suspicious. It honestly never even occurred to me that she might have me followed.'

He looked at me steadily and then at Penny. 'I love Daniel, but I still love my wife. I don't want to hurt either of them. But . . . I have to be true to myself. Whoever or whatever that is. I'm going to have to make a decision, aren't I? Before we get to Bath. I have to decide who or what is really important to me.'

'What do you think you're going to decide?' I said.

Rupert smiled sadly. 'I haven't got a clue. All I can be sure of is that, whatever I do, someone's going to be hurt. Almost certainly me. All I really get to decide is who else I'm going to hurt.'

Penny put a hand on my arm, and I nodded. 'Thank you, Rupert. I think that's enough for now.'

'Are you sure?' said Rupert. He looked too worn out even to feel relieved the questioning was over. 'We haven't talked about Sir Dennis.'

'You've given us more than enough to think about for the moment, Rupert,' said Penny.

He got up and went back to his seat. Sita and Howard looked at him enquiringly, but he had nothing to say.

'Well,' said Penny, 'that was interesting. But not terribly useful.'

'It turns out the problem isn't getting these people to open up, after all,' I said. 'It's getting them to *stop* talking. And what secrets they do have don't seem to have any connection to Sir Dennis.'

'None of them feel like professional killers,' said Penny. 'Or clever enough to have worked out a way to get past us to Sir Dennis, without us noticing. If there was anyone else in this carriage to point a finger at, I'd clear all of them as suspects. But where does that leave us? Back with the invisible psychic assassin?'

'I still don't believe in him,' I said.

'Maybe that's what he wants you to think,' said Penny.

'Really not helping . . .'

And then we both looked round sharply as Sita suddenly launched herself up out of her seat and came striding down the aisle. She shot Penny and me a brief contemptuous glare as she stalked past us, before finally slamming to a halt right in front of Brian, still standing guard at the door. I didn't make any move to stop Sita – partly because I thought I could trust Brian to keep his mouth shut, but mostly because I was interested in what Sita might have to say. Brian looked at her coldly.

'What do you want?'

'Just to talk,' said Sita.

'I don't talk to reporters,' said Brian.

'Why not?' said Sita. 'Got something to hide?'

She tried to say it lightly, but that wasn't how it came out. Brian moved forward, and Sita quickly retreated a step.

'You should go back to your seat,' said Brian. 'And mind your own damn business.'

'Why?' said Sita. 'What is it you're afraid I might ask?'

'I'm not afraid of anything,' said Brian, pulling himself up to his full height. And then wincing despite himself as his injured knee complained. 'Least of all a muckraker like you.'

'Come on, Brian,' said Sita, doing her best to smile winningly. 'You must have some idea of what's really going on. You were Sir Dennis's official bodyguard. What made him suddenly so important? And why was he in so much danger that he needed someone like you to protect him?'

Brian just looked at her. Sita waited, bouncing impatiently on her toes, until she realized he had no intention of saying anything, and then she made an angry sound, turned round and stomped back to her seat. She'd gambled on bypassing me and Penny in the hope of getting more information out of Brian, and now she'd failed in front of everyone. She threw herself back into her seat and scowled angrily out of the window, so she wouldn't have to look at anyone else.

A thought occurred to me, and I left my seat. Penny started to get up, but I gestured for her to stay where she was and keep a careful eye on everyone. I made my way down the aisle to where Rupert was sitting. He saw me coming and rose quickly from his seat to stand in the aisle and face me.

'None of what's happened is anything to do with me!' he said loudly. 'Why can't you just leave me alone? There's nothing more I can tell you. Why do you keep hounding me when there's a professional killer on this train?'

'He has a point,' Howard said mildly.

'Damn right!' said Sita. 'You tell him, Rupert!'

Rupert glared right into my face, so angry now he was actually trembling with the force of his emotions.

'You must have some idea who was after Sir Dennis! Is the killer some kind of terrorist? Is that what all this is about?' And then he stopped abruptly, as he realized what he'd just said. 'A terrorist . . . Is there a bomb on this train?'

'Calm down, Rupert,' I said. 'I just wanted to ask you . . .'

But he'd already turned away from me. 'Everybody! Listen to me! There could be a bomb on this train!'

Rupert's gaze lit upon the communication cord, and he lunged towards it. I had to grab him by the shoulder and haul him back. He fought me fiercely, desperate to get to the cord, until I had no choice but to bearhug him. His legs buckled as all the breath shot out of his lungs, until I was the only thing holding him up. I eased him back into his seat, patted him on the shoulder and then turned around to address the rest of the compartment in my most reassuring voice.

'There's no need for anyone to panic. There is no bomb planted anywhere on this train.'

'You can't be sure of that!' said Sita. She looked genuinely worried. 'You haven't had time to search the whole train.'

'I can be absolutely certain there isn't any bomb,' I said patiently. 'Because if there was, the killer wouldn't have needed to kill Sir Dennis personally, would he?'

There was a pause as everyone considered that, and then all three of them started nodding as they realized that made sense.

'Sorry,' said Rupert. 'Oh, God, I'm so sorry. Of course you're right. It was just . . . Once I got the idea in my head, I couldn't get rid of it. And it finally felt as if there was something I could do . . .'

'Now that's a feeling I can appreciate,' I said. 'But even if you had pulled the cord, it wouldn't have made any difference.'

'Why not?' Sita said immediately.

'Because this is a special express,' I said. 'The driver has strict instructions not to stop for anything.'

Rupert looked at me disbelievingly. 'But . . . what if we really needed to stop? What if there was a medical emergency?'

'I didn't hurt you that badly,' I said.

'You know what I mean! What if the killer decided to strike again, and one of us got hurt?'

They all saw the answer to that in my face.

'Typical security,' Sita said bitterly. 'You people don't give a damn what happens to the innocent bystanders, as long as you get your man.'

'As long as the killer is still on the loose, we're all in danger,' I said steadily. 'By concentrating on finding him, I'm working to protect all of you.'

'You'd say anything, wouldn't you?' Rupert said sullenly. 'To get us to do what you want.'

Penny hurried down the aisle and knelt beside him. 'Would you like me to sit with you, Rupert? Keep you company, till you've calmed down a bit?'

'I'd rather be on my own,' he said stiffly. 'I don't trust you. Either of you. My private life is my business, and if I don't want to talk about it, I shouldn't have to. You have no right to bully me! Nothing that's happened on this train is anything to do with me, and I don't want anything to do with it.'

He turned away and stared determinedly out of the window at the darkness beyond. Sita applauded loudly, and Howard looked as if he wanted to. Penny stood up and looked at me. I shrugged, and we walked back to our seats.

'What was it you were going to ask him?' said Penny.

'Nothing worth upsetting him that much. I just wanted to check whether his boyfriend might be connected to Sir Dennis in some way.'

'That's a bit of a long shot, isn't it?'

'It's not as if we have any other leads worth pursuing.'

Penny lowered her voice. 'If the communication cord wouldn't work, why did you have to go to such lengths to prevent Rupert from pulling it?'

'Because I couldn't be sure that the driver really would ignore an actual emergency call,' I said quietly. 'At least now we can be certain that none of the others will try it.'

Penny looked at me sharply. 'That's cold, Ishmael.'

I shrugged. 'Rupert isn't the only one who's feeling a bit frustrated. Look, why don't you go and sit with Sita for a bit? See what you can get out of her, when I'm not there for her to disapprove of. I'll have another word with Howard. I have a feeling he might open up a bit more if it's just me.'

'What am I supposed to say to Sita?' said Penny.

'I don't know,' I said. 'Girl talk?' I caught the expression forming on Penny's face and hurried on. 'I've been wondering whether she was supposed to overhear all that political stuff at Westminster. See if the same thought had occurred to her, and if so, how much of it she thinks we can trust.'

Penny nodded reluctantly and went over to Sita. The young journalist scowled at her suspiciously, but grudgingly allowed Penny to sit down. I left them to it and went to stand next to Howard. He looked up at me wearily.

'What now, Mr Jones?'

'Just a few more questions,' I said. 'Shall we move down the aisle a little, away from curious ears?'

Howard nodded resignedly and got to his feet. Of all the people in the carriage, he struck me as the least affected by everything that had happened. He didn't even appear that bothered about being questioned again. We made our way further along the aisle and sat down opposite each other, and he looked at me as though he was just waiting for this new intrusion to be over, so he could go back to thinking about whatever it was that was so important to him.

'Won't Penny be joining us this time?' said Howard. 'I like Penny.'

'She's very likeable,' I said. 'I thought you and I should have a quiet word on our own, Howard, because sometimes we can say things to a stranger that we could never say to anyone we know. As long as there aren't any witnesses.'

He just looked at me.

'You're keeping something from me, Howard,' I said. 'And I need to know what it is.'

He managed a small smile. 'I would have thought everyone in this compartment was keeping something from you.'

I nodded, acknowledging the point. 'I need to find out what it is you're concealing from me, Howard, if only so I can stop worrying about it.'

'But what if it's something I don't want to talk about?' said Howard, meeting my gaze unflinchingly. 'What if it's just none of your business?'

'In a murder enquiry, everything has to be my business,' I said. 'Because I can never be sure what might turn out to be connected to the killer or their motivations. Look, if your secret really does turn out to be nothing to do with what's going on here, I promise I'll keep it strictly to myself. I won't even tell Penny.'

Howard sat stiffly in his seat, completely unmoved. 'I have nothing to say to you. And there's nothing you can threaten me with, Mr Security Man Jones. I'm not afraid of you, or whatever authorities you really represent.'

'No,' I said, 'you really aren't, are you? And that . . . is interesting. Everyone else is at least a bit intimidated by me, or the thought of whom I might represent. And they're all more than a bit worried that one of their fellow passengers might turn out to be the murderer. But you don't even give a damn about that, do you, Howard?'

He shrugged. 'I didn't see or hear anything. I'm not a suspect or a witness. None of this is anything to do with me.'

'No,' I said. 'That's not it. That's not why you're so . . . unconnected from everything that's going on.'

'I just want to be left alone,' said Howard.

'That's what everyone wants,' I said. 'Unfortunately, the situation doesn't give a damn what we want. I have to get to the truth or the murderer could get away, and I can't let that happen.'

He shrugged again. 'Sorry.'

'No,' I said. 'I really don't think you are. I don't think any of this affects you in the least, Howard, because you're only thinking about one thing.'

He stared back at me, saying nothing. I sat back in my seat and considered him carefully. Howard was holding himself perfectly still, and had been ever since he sat down. Not because he was worried or hostile . . . but because it was taking all his strength and concentration to hold himself together, so he wouldn't give anything away.

'What could be so important,' I said finally, 'that you're ready to let a cold-blooded killer escape rather than talk about it? Perhaps I should have brought Penny with me after all; she's the one with the people skills. But you see, Howard, I have the advantage that comes from being an outsider. I've spent most of my life pretending to be just like everyone else, when I'm really not. And I've put so much effort into constructing an everyday mask to hide behind that I've learned to see past everyone else's. So what have I learned, Howard, from studying you?

'You don't care that Sir Dennis was killed. You don't care about my questions. You're not scared of the murderer or the situation you're in, which makes you unique in this compartment. Add to that . . . your mind is always somewhere else, preoccupied with something you're planning to do, once you get to Bath. The one time you stood up to me was when you were concerned you might not get there on time. So I have to wonder, Howard, what could be so important to you that you can't think of anything else, even when your life could be in danger?'

Howard met my gaze steadily, his face completely unmoved. We might have been talking about the weather.

'It's just something I have to do,' he said.

'And what then?'

'I don't understand.'

'What will you do after you've done this very important thing, Howard?'

He seemed genuinely lost for words for a moment. In the end, he just produced another of his shrugs.

'Then . . . it'll be done. I won't have to think about it any more.'

'Ah . . .' I said. 'I was afraid of that. I'm sorry, Howard, but you're really not very good at concealing the truth, while I am very good at getting to the bottom of things. Now I've put all the clues together, there is only one conclusion that makes sense. Tell me, Howard, how long have you been planning to kill yourself?'

His eyes opened wide, and his jaw dropped as though he'd been hit. And then he let out all his breath in a long sigh and slumped back in his seat as all the strength went out of him. He looked suddenly older, and worn out, as though I'd kicked away the last crutch that had been holding him up. He smiled at me tiredly, with perhaps just a little bit of relief in it, now he no longer had to pretend.

'Oh, hell . . . why not? Why not tell the truth and shame the devil? What difference can it make? What does any of it matter now?' He nodded to himself for a moment, gathering his thoughts, and then he leaned forward and fixed me with a defiant look.

'I haven't been entirely honest with you, because I didn't think my life was any of your business. But you're never going to leave any of us alone until you've revealed all our secrets. And to hell with who it hurts. Very well, then; this is my secret. And damn you to hell for making me say it.

'My wife is dead. I lost my Annie when I lost my job, because of Sir Dennis and his interference. I didn't find another job, because it turned out there was a glut of people like me on the market, and most of the others were a lot younger than me. What was I supposed to do? I didn't know anything else.

'We ran through our savings in under a year. We were going to lose the house. Annie loved that house. It was all we had; she never wanted children. She died at the end of last year. She wasn't ill; I think by then she was just so tired, and so frightened of the future, that she simply decided she didn't want to live any more. I blame myself for her death. I promised Annie I'd always look after her, and I didn't.'

'So that's why you got on this train?' I said. 'To confront Sir Dennis, the man responsible for your wife's death.'

Howard looked at me as though I was mad. 'No. I didn't know he was going to be here. I'm going to Bath so I can go back to the hotel where Annie and I spent our honeymoon, all those years ago. I was able to book the very same room. We were so happy then. We had no idea how our lives were going to turn out. I'm going to sit in that room, look out at the view and then kill myself. Because that's the only way I can be with her again.'

He glared at me openly, defying me to feel sorry for him. 'Do you want to see my bottle of pills? Or the razor blade?'

He undid his left cuff and pulled back his jacket and shirt sleeve, to show me his forearm. It was covered with cut marks. Some were old, little more than scars, while the most recent were still red and angry. None of them were more than two or three inches long, criss-crossing each other in a vicious, ugly pattern. Howard turned his arm back and forth, to make sure I got a good look.

'The technical term is self-harming, but I like to think of them as practice. Learning how much willpower and self-control it takes to cut into your own skin. To not care about the pain or mind about the blood. I went online first, to check out the details. There are all kinds of helpful sites. Did you know that if you cut across your wrists, there's always the chance your blood will clot and keep you alive long enough for some well-meaning fool to save you? If you want to be sure – I mean *really* sure – you have to cut the length of the vein from the wrist up to the elbow. No one's going to save you after that. And I don't want to be saved.'

He pulled his shirt and jacket sleeves back down and looked at me coldly.

'I would prefer to go out peacefully, with some dignity, but one way or another I'm going. You want to know what I was writing on my laptop? My suicide note. It's harder than you think to sum up a lifetime's regrets in just a few words. In the end, all I had was that I just don't want to do this any more.'

Howard finally ground to a halt and fixed me with a burning gaze, demanding a response.

'You can't just give up,' I said finally. 'Life can always surprise you.'

'Take your platitudes and shove them,' said Howard. 'You know, it's actually very liberating when you decide your life is over . . . You don't have to give a shit what anyone thinks. All that matters is that I'm going to be with my wife again, and you can't stop me!'

I looked around the compartment. Everyone was staring at us. Howard's voice had risen to the point where they couldn't help but overhear. Penny was already hurrying down the aisle to join us. I was relieved. I had no idea what to say to Howard. Penny crouched down beside him.

'What was your wife's name, Howard?' she said quietly.

'Annie,' he said.

'Is this . . . what you're planning to do . . . is this what Annie would have wanted you to do?'

'I don't know,' said Howard. 'And I don't care.'

And then he started crying and couldn't stop. Penny put a comforting arm across his shoulders.

'Let it out, Howard,' she said gently. 'And we'll give you some time alone. I need to talk to Ishmael, but we won't be far away if you need anything.'

Howard just nodded. I think we all knew he was past the point where even the most well-meant words of comfort would help. I got up out of my seat, and Penny and I moved off down the aisle.

'Are you all right?' she said quietly.

'Not really,' I said. 'You know that wasn't what I wanted.'

'I know.'

'I didn't pressure him into a confession,' I said. 'I just worked it out, by listening to what he didn't say.'

Penny shook her head. 'You're good at getting to the truth, Ishmael, but you don't always think enough about the collateral damage.'

'We're running out of time,' I said. 'And we still aren't any nearer working out who the murderer is.'

'I think we can safely assume it isn't Howard,' said Penny.

'Can we?' I said. 'Who'd make a better killer than a man who honestly doesn't care whether or not he gets caught?'

'You don't really mean that, Ishmael.'

I nodded reluctantly. 'Either he's the best actor I've ever seen or he's in no fit state to commit a murder. And I don't think anyone's that good an actor.'

'You won't get any more out of him for a while,' said Penny. 'Poor man. Maybe we can get him some help when we get to Bath.'

I shook my head helplessly. 'Every time I figure out what one of our suspects is keeping from us, it turns out to be nothing to do with Sir Dennis or his killer.'

'There is one person left that you haven't talked to,' said Penny.

She nodded at Brian, still standing guard at the door and glaring suspiciously at everyone else.

'I know,' I said. 'I've been putting it off, because once I've talked to him . . . I don't have anywhere else to go.'

'Talk to the man,' said Penny. 'He must know something.'

'Oh, I'm sure he knows something,' I said. 'But what are the odds it'll turn out to be anything useful?'

Penny looked at me, not quite smiling. 'Do you want me to come with you and hold your hand?'

'Better not,' I said. 'He wouldn't respect me then.'

'I'm not sure he does now,' said Penny.

I made my way down the aisle. Brian saw me coming, and his scowl actually deepened. I gestured for him to stand aside, so I could look through the glass partition in the door. He did so reluctantly, as though in giving up his position he was surrendering what little authority he had left. I stared through the vestibule to the darkness in the next carriage, reassuring myself we were still cut off from the rest of the train.

'There's no one out there,' said Brian. 'I've been keeping an eye. Can I be blunt, Mr Special Bodyguard?'

I turned back to face him. 'I'd be shocked if you were anything else.'

I could see he was disappointed that I hadn't objected, so he could justify being angry with me. I gave him my most polite smile, just to annoy him.

'What's on your mind, Brian?'

'I've been thinking,' he said. 'I've been a military policeman for almost eight years now, and I've seen enough evil in men that I really can't bring myself to buy into any of this psychic nonsense. What I saw on the cover of Sir Dennis's file must have been code for something else, and I think it's about time you told me what. I need to know what's really going on, so I know what to look for.'

'Sorry, Brian,' I said. 'Sometimes . . . things just are what they are, whether we want them to be or not.'

'Don't feed me that bullshit!' Brian said loudly. 'If you don't want to tell me the truth, you don't have to, but don't insult my intelligence.'

'Wouldn't dream of it,' I said. 'Can we talk about Sir Dennis now?'

He glowered at me fiercely. 'You've talked to everyone else and got nowhere, so now you're left talking to me. But I did everything I was supposed to. Sir Dennis only died because he was stupid enough to ignore his own bodyguard! You're not pinning anything on me, just because you can't find the real murderer!'

He lashed out at me so suddenly that I honestly didn't see it coming. My reflexes sent me stumbling backwards the moment he started moving, but the punch still hit my nose hard enough to drive my head back. I raised my hands to defend myself and only then realized that Brian had lost all interest in attacking me. His face had gone deathly pale, and his eyes were wide with shock.

I started toward him and he backed quickly away. The door hissed open behind him and he stumbled back into the vestibule, making awkward warding-off gestures with his hands, as though he was facing some kind of monster. I stopped where I was.

'What is wrong with you, Brian?'

'Stay where you are,' he said hoarsely. 'Don't come any closer. What the hell are you?'

'I already told you,' I said. 'I'm security.'

'But what else are you?' said Brian. His voice was choked with horror.

I felt something touch my upper lip. I put my hand to my nose, and when I took it away my fingertips had golden blood on them. The blow to my nose must have connected more solidly than I'd realized. I took out a handkerchief and pressed it to my nostrils, stopping the bleeding. I cleaned my nose and upper lip carefully, put the handkerchief away and looked steadily at Brian.

'Get back in here. Don't make me have to come and get you.'

Brian came slowly back into the compartment, never taking his eyes off me until the door slid shut behind him.

'No one else saw anything,' I said quietly. 'And you didn't either. Is that understood?'

'Got it,' said Brian. He swallowed hard. 'I didn't see anything.'

'And you can't tell anyone else about this. Is that clear, Brian?'

'Who would I tell?' Brian said numbly. 'Who would believe me?'

'That's the spirit,' I said. 'Now, stay here and guard this door, until I tell you otherwise.'

I started to turn away.

'What are you?' said Brian.

'Undercover,' I said.

I went back down the aisle, to where Penny and Sita were chatting happily together. I dropped on to the seat facing them, and they both stopped talking, exchanged a look and burst out laughing.

'Are you all right, darling?' said Penny, once she could control herself. 'That punch did look as if it might have been a bit painful.'

'It was only a glancing blow,' I said, with as much dignity as I could manage. 'I think he just needed to get it out of his system.'

'Are you ready now to tell me who you really work for?' said Sita. 'And don't try to fob me off with that security crap. It might work on anyone else, but I've been around. What department are we talking about? What's your remit, and who gives you your orders? I know I can't write about it, but I still need to know if I'm going to trust you.'

'You must have heard rumours,' I said. 'About departments within departments, that don't officially exist.'

'Oh . . .' said Sita. 'So you work for one of those?'

'Of course not,' I said. 'They don't exist, remember?'

Sita gave me a withering look and turned to Penny.

'You want the truth?' Penny said calmly. 'All right, then. Ishmael and I work for an organization so secret it doesn't have a name. Even we have no idea who they are or what they're for.'

Sita glared at her. 'I know when I'm being patronized.' She jumped to her feet and strode off in a huff, dropping moodily into another seat some distance away.

'You tell them the truth and they still won't believe you,' said Penny.

'We should try that more often,' I said. 'Can I just ask: what were the two of you cackling about so companionably?'

Penny grinned. 'How much Sita wanted to punch you on the nose, like Brian did. I told her I often feel the same way.' She glanced back at Brian. 'Something freaked him out there. What happened?'

'He made my nose bleed,' I said. 'Just for a moment.'

Penny's mouth made a small *Oh!* of understanding, and she leaned quickly forward to check there was no blood left on my face.

'Hold it,' I said. 'Sita's up to something.'

'Now what?' said Penny.

Sita was back up on her feet again, commanding the middle of the aisle. She glared at Penny and me, and raised her voice to address the whole compartment.

'We can't let those two order us around! We have no idea who they really are, or who they work for. They have no authority over us!'

'What do you suggest we do about it?' Rupert said mildly. 'We're trapped on the train with them, all the way to Bath.'

Sita stabbed a finger at him triumphantly. 'You had the right idea. Pull the communication cord and stop the train. Then just sit tight until the proper authorities can get here and take over.'

'But according to Mr Jones, pulling the cord won't make any difference,' said Howard. 'The driver has orders not to stop for anything.'

'And you believe him?' said Sita.

'Why would he lie to us?' said Rupert.

'Why do you think?' said Sita.

She smiled at me defiantly and lunged for the cord, but Brian had moved quietly down the aisle and was already in position to block the way with his body. Sita scowled at him, and he smiled back at her.

'Get out of the way, Brian.'

'Sit down, Sita.'

'And what if I don't choose to take orders from a hired thug like you?' said Sita.

Brian's smile widened. 'Then I'll just have to make you do what you're told, won't I?'

Sita went to dodge round him, one outstretched arm straining for the cord, but Brian grabbed a handful of her jacket and hauled her up short. She fought to break free of him, and Brian couldn't hold on to her, so he threw her to the floor. She cried out as she sprawled helplessly on all fours. I was down the aisle and on top of Brian before he had time to react. I picked him up with one hand and threw him the length of the compartment. He hurtled ungainly through the air and finally hit the floor hard enough to drive all the breath out of him.

It was suddenly very quiet. Everyone watched wide-eyed as I walked unhurriedly down the aisle to stand over Brian. He was already struggling to get to his feet again, but one look at me was enough to put a stop to that.

'I was only doing my job,' he said.

'From now on, your job is to do nothing except what I tell you to do,' I said coldly. 'So get up, go back to the door and, whatever happens, stay there. Leave the passengers alone.'

Brian got to his feet, pulled his clothes back into place and looked at me uncertainly. I don't think he'd ever been handled that casually before. He leaned forward, lowering his voice so no one else would hear us.

'I know what you are now. You're one of those psychic people, aren't you?'

'Guard the door, Brian.'

He brushed past me and limped off down the aisle. He stepped carefully around Sita, went straight to the end door, put his back to it and stared straight ahead. Penny helped Sita to her feet, but Sita immediately jerked free of her and went back to her seat, without looking at Penny or me. Rupert and Howard looked at each other and said nothing. I raised my voice, to make sure everyone would hear me.

'We will be arriving in Bath in about thirty minutes. Anyone who wants to make an official complaint can talk to the authorities then. You can wait that long, can't you? Now please, all of you . . . just stay put where you are, and let Penny and me get on with our investigation.'

'Of course,' Sita said bitterly. 'Because you've done such a great job so far, haven't you?'

'You're still alive, aren't you?' I said.

She wouldn't look at me. Neither would Brian. Howard and Rupert said nothing. Penny moved in beside me.

'All right,' she said quietly. 'Now what are we going to do?'

'Damned if I know,' I said. 'But we've got less than thirty minutes to think of something.'

FIVE

Trapped in the Pressure Cooker

I went back to my seat by the door, carefully ignoring Brian, sat down and stared at nothing. Penny sat beside me, not saying anything, allowing me to concentrate. Further down the carriage, I could see Rupert and Howard and Sita sitting in their separate seats, not even glancing at each other, all of them lost in their own thoughts.

It was quiet in the First-Class compartment. A very strained quiet, that no one wanted to break. The train sped on towards Bath, and there was nothing outside the windows but the night. I sat still, frowning hard, trying to find some new way to attack a problem that refused to be solved. I had to be missing something, but I was damned if I could see what.

I studied the three passengers carefully, taking my time. None of them struck me as a killer, let alone the professional assassin I'd been warned about. But none of that mattered, because none of them could possibly have done it. They were all sitting in their seats, right in front of me, while Sir Dennis was being killed. They couldn't have got past me.

Sir Dennis had been a real pain in the arse while he was alive, and being murdered hadn't changed that one bit.

There was always the chance that someone was messing with my head. Which meant I had to re-examine the possibility of a hidden psychic assassin. The evidence – what there was of it – seemed to be forcing me in that direction. But I hadn't observed any of the usual psychic fallout, the odd events and strange coincidences that should have accompanied a psychic exercising his powers. And I was still certain I would know he was there, no matter how well he hid himself.

Because no psychic had ever been able to hide himself from me.

But I'd never come up against a really powerful rogue. I looked slowly around the compartment, taking in the apparently empty seats. Could the killer really be sitting there, hiding behind the power of his monstrous mind, watching me flounder about and get nowhere . . . and smiling? And if so, was there any way I could force or trick him into revealing himself? I thought about that for a while . . . And a cold hand clutched at my heart as I suddenly realized there was one way. One simple, direct and extremely dangerous way.

All I had to do was lower the defensive routines operating in the back of my mind, and leave my thoughts open for the rogue psychic to read. He had to be feeling frustrated at not being able to read my mind. He shouldn't be able to resist taking a look. If nothing else, he must want to know whether or not I suspected his presence. So if I left my mind wide open, and let him in, and he saw the truth of who and what I really was, the shock of finding out I wasn't actually human ought to be enough to shatter his concentration and make him drop his invisibility, if only for a moment. And then I would be able to see him, and I would know.

It didn't matter how powerful his mind was; he was still only human. And I could use my more-than-human speed to get to him before he could do anything to me.

But if I did decide to drop all my defences, that would mean revealing my secrets not only to the rogue but potentially also to the Division psychics watching over the train. According to Mr Nobody, the Division was fascinated by the Organization and desperate to learn all they could about its field agents. If the watching psychics thought they could get away with it, without being noticed, would they be tempted? Would a gentlemen's agreement really be enough to keep them out of my mind? And if the Division found out who and what I was, what would they do with that information? Pressure me to work for them, instead of the Organization? Or, since they were a part of the Government, would they feel obliged to turn me in?

My hands were clutching the seat's arm rests so fiercely they ached. I was so tense I could hardly breathe. I'd spent decades hiding the secret of my existence from the world. Was

I really ready to give it up, just for a chance at taking down a professional assassin? It wasn't as if he'd killed anyone who mattered. No one was going to miss a corrupt scumbag like Sir Dennis. If I lowered my defences, I could be putting my life in danger, or at the very least throwing my freedom away for nothing . . .

No, not for nothing. To prevent a killer from getting away. I couldn't put my own needs first. That wasn't the kind of man I was, the kind of man I'd chosen to be. I couldn't live with myself if I stopped being that man.

I turned to Penny and quietly explained what I had in mind. She started shaking her head almost immediately and put a staying hand on my arm, but I just kept talking, quietly and reasonably. When I finally stopped, she had her answer ready, carefully keeping her voice calm and controlled.

'This is a really bad idea, Ishmael. Even if the Division psychics do follow the rules and stay out of your head, you can't depend on the rogue just taking a quick look. What if he decides to attack your mind while he has the chance?'

'I'll just have to risk it,' I said steadily. 'And trust my hidden self to fight him off. I'd back that scary bastard against any psychic. Either way, I have to do this, Penny. I can't risk letting the killer getting away. God knows how many more people he might kill before he is finally brought down, and I can't have that on my conscience. So I need you to keep a careful eye on the empty seats while I do this. Watch for even the briefest glimpse of someone sitting where no one should be. You won't be in any danger; the rogue will be too occupied with me to even notice you.'

'No, wait a minute, please . . . Think this through, Ishmael.' Penny was clutching my arm with both hands now, her gaze fixed desperately on mine. 'Even if you can surprise the rogue into revealing himself, what then?'

'Then I'll deal with him.'

'How?'

'The same way I deal with any threat,' I said. 'I'll jump him before he can react, and punch him repeatedly in the head until he's so unconscious even his powers won't be able to wake him up. Once we get to Bath, we just hand him over to the authorities and let them handle him.'

'But what if, when we arrive at Bath, the authorities aren't just there for him?' Penny said urgently. 'What if the Division psychics pass on what they've discovered about you, and the authorities are there to grab you as well? You can't rely on the Organization to protect an alien passing as human.' And then she stopped as a new thought struck her. 'Unless . . . Ishmael, do you suppose the Organization knows what you really are, and has done all along?'

'I have wondered that, from time to time,' I said. 'The Organization and I get along perfectly well not asking questions and respecting each other's secrets. But you're quite right; they wouldn't fight for me. I'm just a field agent, an expendable asset; I've always known that.'

'After everything you've done for them?'

'That's just the job,' I said. 'That's always been the job, whichever underground group I've worked for. Penny, I have to try this. Because if there is a rogue psychic in here with us, I don't know any other way to stop him.'

Penny smiled suddenly. 'And you wonder if you're really human. You care about other people, darling. What could be more human than that?'

'Keep a careful watch,' I said. Because right then I couldn't trust myself to say anything else.

I settled back in my seat, trying to get comfortable, if not actually relaxed. I closed my eyes and looked inwards, checking my mental protections were still in place. The old routines, quietly running themselves in a constant murmur at the back of my thoughts, that I couldn't normally hear. Slowly, deliberately, I shut down my protections, layer by layer, and the murmur grew fainter and fainter until finally it stopped. I tried to ignore how fast my heart was beating and sat very still. I felt horribly exposed and vulnerable – like a goat staked out in a jungle clearing, waiting for the tiger to come and get it.

I braced myself, though I wasn't sure against what. I had no idea what a telepathic invasion would feel like. I still had no sense, no feeling, that there was a psychic anywhere near me. There were no strange voices in my head, no unexpected thoughts or impulses, not even a deep-down suspicion that I might not be alone in the dark. I slowly opened my eyes and looked around the compartment. There wasn't even a flicker of an unexpected presence in any of the empty seats. Nothing to suggest a tiger was lurking in the undergrowth. I started my protective routines running again, slamming each layer back into place as quickly as I could, sealing my mind off from all outside thoughts and influences. Until finally I could relax again.

I was breathing hard, and so exhausted I could barely move. A cold sweat had beaded on my face. Penny mopped it away with a handkerchief, looking at me anxiously, and I managed a smile for her.

'I'm back. And I'm still me. No unwelcome visitations inside my head. Did you see anything?'

'No, Ishmael. And I looked really hard.'

'While I didn't get any sense of another presence . . .' I stretched slowly, easing the aches in my muscles as the tension fell slowly away.

'Can we can be sure now that there isn't a rogue psychic in here with us?' said Penny.

'I don't see how he could have avoided giving himself away,' I said. 'It's not every day you encounter an alien from outer space travelling on a London train.'

Penny looked round sharply. 'Ishmael! Sita's on the move again.'

I sighed. 'That woman is more trouble than everyone else put together.'

'Of course. She's a journalist.'

Sita went striding determinedly down the aisle, to loom over Rupert. He looked up, startled, as she dropped into the seat opposite him and leaned forward, gesturing sharply for him to do the same. Once their heads were almost touching, Sita murmured fiercely to him for some time. Then they both sat back in their seats and looked at me suspiciously. I made sure I just happened to be looking somewhere else. Sita and Rupert got to their feet and went to join Howard. He looked at them coldly when they sat down facing him, making it clear he wasn't interested in anything they had to say. But once again Sita leaned forward and murmured urgently, and after a while Howard started nodding, if a little reluctantly.

Penny leaned in beside me. 'What do you suppose is going on there?'

'I don't know,' I said. 'Looks like Sita's had a new idea. I'd better find out what she's up to.'

'Like she'd tell you anything,' said Penny.

'I wasn't planning on asking her,' I said. 'I'll just crank up my hearing and listen in on what they're saying. You keep an eye on Brian; make sure he doesn't get up to anything unfortunate while I'm preoccupied. But please, don't speak to me unless it's urgent; I'm going to have to really concentrate.'

'You and your weird senses,' said Penny.

I watched Sita and Rupert and Howard carefully, as I opened my hearing up to more-than-human levels. Most of the time I keep it cranked down low, so the sheer noise of the world won't overwhelm me. I carefully faded out the sounds of Penny sitting next to me, the rustle of her clothing as she moved, the steady rhythms of her breathing. And then I did the same with Brian. Finally, I shut out all the noises of the train: the distant roar of the engine, the wheels on the tracks. I focused only on what the three passengers were saying . . . and their voices came to me perfectly clearly, as though I was sitting right there with them.

I studied their faces closely as well, because the words of a conversation don't tell you everything.

All three were bent forward in their seats, their heads close together. Sita looked intense and utterly convinced by what she was saying. Rupert looked interested but sceptical. Howard looked detached and only slightly intrigued. But the more Sita talked, the more the other two wanted to listen.

'We have to do something!' she said urgently. 'Jones and his partner still see us as suspects!'

'Isn't that their job?' Howard said mildly. 'They're investigating a murder, and we're the only ones who could have done it.'

'Are we?' Sita said immediately. 'Really? Jones has already

admitted there's no way we could have sneaked past him and Penny to get to Sir Dennis without either of them noticing.'

'If they're trying to find a killer,' said Rupert, 'doesn't that mean we have a duty to cooperate? We don't want the killer to escape.'

'But that's only if they are what they say they are,' Sita said darkly. 'And I'm not convinced about that. We know they're not police, just security – whatever that means . . . What if they're not really here to identify the killer, but just to cover up what happened? Because the Government would find it too embarrassing, to have to admit that the new head of an important division could be killed so easily. It would be so much better for them if they could pretend none of this ever happened, and Sir Dennis just died of a heart attack or something.'

'I love the way your mind works,' said Howard.

'What has all of this got to do with us?' said Rupert.

'Think about it!' said Sita. 'If this does turn into a cover-up, Jones and Penny won't want us telling anyone the truth, will they?'

'But we'll be arriving in Bath soon,' said Howard. 'They can't stop us talking after that.'

'I'll be glad to get off this train,' said Rupert. 'This whole journey has been nothing but one nightmare after another.'

'How many times do I have to say this before it sinks in?' Sita said urgently. 'They're not police; they're security – and we're in their power!' Her voice was cold and grim now. 'What if they decide to have us arrested in Bath? What if someone then decides it would be in the Government's best interests if we just disappeared? So we couldn't contradict the official version of what happened here?'

'You're reaching now,' said Howard.

'Am I?' said Sita.

'Yes,' Rupert said firmly.

Sita looked at their faces and realized she'd lost them.

'All right, maybe they wouldn't go that far . . . But we still can't trust Jones or Penny! We have to do something, to make it clear to them we're not going to just roll over and go along with whatever they say.'

'What did you have in mind?' said Howard.

'What can we do?' said Rupert.

'We can insist on being allowed to go and sit in another carriage, with the rest of the passengers,' said Sita. 'If we all stick together and stand up to them, they can't stop us walking out of here.'

'What difference would changing carriages make?' said Rupert. 'We'd still be stuck on this train, with a murderer on the loose.'

'I think we'd be a lot safer in another carriage,' said Sita meaningfully.

'How?' said Rupert. 'The killer could still come after us, wherever we are.'

'That's not what she's getting at,' said Howard, looking thoughtfully at Sita. 'If we were sitting among a crowd of witnesses, that means Jones and Penny wouldn't dare touch us.'

'Wait a minute . . . You think they might hurt us?' said Rupert. 'But they're here to protect us, aren't they?'

'Are they?' said Sita.

They all turned around in their seats, so they could get a good look at Penny and me. I looked away the moment I saw their heads start to turn, and waited for them to start talking again before I turned back.

'You really think they might . . . do something to us?' said Rupert. 'Even though they've admitted there's no evidence any of us is the killer?'

'People like them don't need evidence,' Sita said darkly. 'It's always going to be about whatever they can justify as necessary. I'm starting to think there's a lot more going on here than we're being told.'

'How do you mean?' said Howard. For the first time, he was starting to sound genuinely interested in the situation, rather than his own dark thoughts.

'I already told you I cover the political scene for the *Standard*,' said Sita. 'So trust me when I say there's simply no honest way a shifty little creep like Sir Dennis could have been properly appointed head of an important military department. The only way he could have got a top job like that was if there was a fix.'

'What kind of fix?' said Rupert. He was frowning hard as he struggled to keep up with Sita's thinking.

'I haven't worked that out yet,' said Sita. She sounded more embarrassed than angry at being forced to admit there was something she didn't know. 'But given that it's my business to know things like that, or at least be in a position to make an educated guess, the fix must have come from somewhere really high up. That must be why Jones and Penny are here, and it's why we can't trust them. We have no way of knowing what secret instructions they might have been given.'

Sita watched Rupert and Howard closely as they sat silently, working through the implications of what she was telling them. I was impressed at how much of the truth Sita had worked out on her own. She was drawing completely the wrong conclusions, but only because she didn't have all the facts. And, of course, I couldn't tell her.

'You honestly believe Jones and Penny pose a threat to us?' Howard said finally.

'I thought you didn't care what happened to you?' said Rupert.

'I don't,' said Howard. 'But I am . . . interested.'

'Jones does strike me as something of a hard man,' Rupert said thoughtfully. 'You saw how easily he took down the bodyguard. But I don't think Penny would allow him to do anything bad to us.'

'Don't be naive,' said Sita. 'She works for the same people he does.'

'Right,' said Howard. 'It's just bad cop, good cop.'

'They're hiding things from us,' Sita said flatly. 'And I think we need to find out what.'

'You'll never get either of them to tell you the truth,' said Rupert.

'And even if we do stick together and demand to be allowed to leave, I can't see them going along with it,' said Howard. 'It's not like we can force our way past them.'

'There's always Sir Dennis's bodyguard,' said Sita. 'What if we could get him on our side?'

They all turned to look at Brian, standing guard at the door. He met their gaze for a moment and then looked away, making a show of ignoring them.

'Jones already took him down once,' said Howard.

'Only because he caught Brian by surprise,' said Sita.

'But he's military police,' said Rupert. 'He's not going to turn against people in authority, is he?'

'Let me talk to him,' said Sita. 'He doesn't like Jones; I can tell.'

'I'm pretty sure he doesn't like you either,' said Rupert.

'We all saw him hurt you,' said Howard.

Sita sniffed. 'That was just a scuffle. He knew he was in the wrong there; I saw it in his eyes. Maybe I can use that – make him feel guilty enough to listen to me. I'm sure he knows something about Jones . . . You two stay put, and keep an eye on Jones and Penny.'

'Why?' said Howard.

'What could we do?' said Rupert.

'Just . . . watch them!' said Sita. 'And give me some warning if either of them starts moving!'

She jumped up from her seat and strode down the aisle. Brian watched her approach and stood a little straighter. His expression didn't change, but he was clearly doing his best to be ready for anything. Sita stopped a cautious distance away and faced him steadily.

'Hello, Brian.'

'What do you want now, Reporter?'

'I thought we could talk,' said Sita, giving him what she probably thought was a disarming smile.

'Think again,' said Brian. 'I don't have anything to say to you.'

'Why don't you trust Mr Jones?' Sita said bluntly.

She leaned forward a little, inviting confidentiality. Brian shot a quick glance in my direction, and again I was careful to be looking somewhere else and apparently paying them no attention. I looked back when Brian answered her, his voice low.

'What makes you think I don't trust him?'

'Come on, Brian,' said Sita. 'I can see it in your face, every time you look at him. And it's just as obvious that you're scared of him. Now why is that, Brian? What is there about that man that scares a big tough soldier boy like you?'

'Mr Jones is in charge here,' Brian said steadily. 'I accept his authority, that's all.'

'You haven't answered my question,' said Sita. 'Why don't you trust him?'

'Because he's more than he seems to be,' said Brian. 'He isn't what you think he is.'

'How do you mean?' said Sita. She kept her voice soft as well as low, as though she was more interested in him than his answer. 'Are you saying Jones isn't really a security agent?'

Brian shook his head and said nothing. Sita studied him carefully.

'You're shaking, Brian.'

'No, I'm not.'

'You are. You're actually shaking, just at the thought of what you know about him. What could possibly scare you that badly?'

Brian met her gaze steadily. 'All right, I'm frightened. You would be too, if you knew what I know.'

'Then tell me,' said Sita. 'Maybe if you share what you know . . .'

Brian shook his head firmly. His face was pale, and his lips were pressed together so hard they'd lost all colour. Sita started to reach out a hand to him and then pulled it back again.

'Are you scared of what he might do to you if you went against him? Has he threatened you?'

She stopped. She could tell her questions were going wide of the mark, even if she didn't know why. She looked at him for a moment, choosing her words carefully.

'Brian . . . I can't help you if I don't know what the problem is.'

'You can't help me,' Brian said flatly. 'And why would you want to anyway, Reporter?'

'Because we're all of us in the same boat, in the same carriage. And my name is Sita.'

'There's nothing I can tell you, Sita.'

'But you want to, don't you, Brian? I can tell. You know that what's happening here is wrong.'

'You have no idea what's really going on here,' said Brian. 'And you should be grateful for that.'

Sita looked at him, and I saw a chill go through her as she realized how serious he was.

'What the hell did he do to you, Brian?'

'He put me in my place,' said Brian. 'Look, we have to find Sir Dennis's killer before we get to Bath, and Mr Jones and Penny are the only ones who can do that. They're the experts, so we have to go along.'

'But are they?' said Sita.

Brian looked at her. 'What?'

'Are they really experts?' said Sita. She moved in a little closer, holding his gaze with hers. 'We have no proof they're who or what they claim to be. We don't know who gave them their orders, or what their real agenda might be. You're military police, Brian. You know as well as I do that *security* can mean anything.'

'That's the problem,' said Brian. 'It can mean anything. You're wasting your time, Sita. I can't go against Mr Jones.'

'What do you think is going to happen when this train finally gets to Bath?' said Sita. 'To me and Rupert and Howard, and maybe to you as well? Do you honestly think Jones and Penny will let us just walk away if they haven't found the killer? Do you think being a good soldier will protect you from people like them?'

Brian actually smiled for a moment. 'You reporters do love your conspiracies and cover-ups, don't you?'

'I hate them,' Sita said steadily. 'That's why I work so hard to drag them out into the light, so everyone can see them.'

'Are you always this paranoid?' said Brian. And for the first time he seemed more interested in her than in her answer.

'Mostly,' said Sita. 'And I'm right more often than I'm wrong. What is it you know about Jones, that you don't want to tell me?'

Brian hesitated and then shook his head quickly. 'I can't talk about that. And you wouldn't thank me if I did.'

Sita scowled. 'So many secrets on this train . . . There must be something you can do to help us!'

Brian looked at her thoughtfully. 'I do have a backup weapon.'

'What?'

'I have another gun,' said Brian. He was keeping his voice carefully low, and Sita had to lean in closer to hear him. Brian carefully avoided looking at me as he continued. 'I have a second gun in an ankle holster, on my other leg. My superiors thought I should be prepared for . . . emergencies.'

'Why haven't you used it?' said Sita.

'And do what?' said Brian. 'Even if I was prepared to go up against Jones, and I'm not, he still has my main weapon. Given the atmosphere in this carriage, he'd probably open fire the moment I drew my gun. And besides . . . I'm not convinced a gun would be much use against him anyway.'

Sita looked at him sharply, intrigued by what Brian wasn't saying but which she could still hear in his voice.

'What are you saying, Brian? That Jones has body armour?'

Brian shook his head. 'I just don't see anything useful I could do with a gun.'

'Then give me the gun,' said Sita.

Brian looked at her for a moment and then smiled. 'You've got guts; I'll give you that. But what would you do with a gun, if I did let you have it?'

'I don't know! Protect myself and the other passengers. From the killer, and Jones and Penny. Maybe . . . force Jones to tell us all the truth about what's really going on.'

She broke off. Brian had stopped smiling and was shaking his head.

'You don't want to know what's really going on. Trust me. Anyway, does Jones look the type to be intimidated by a gun?'

Sita scowled. 'Not really, no.'

'He'd just take it away from you,' said Brian. 'I'm keeping my backup weapon until we get to Bath. Just in case the killer reveals himself.'

'And if Jones and Penny turn out to be as much a threat to us as the killer?'

Brian looked at her steadily. 'If push should come to shove, there is a line I won't cross. I would never let him hurt you.'

'Well, that's good to know. Thank you, Brian.'

They looked at each other for a long moment, and then Sita turned away and went back to sit with Rupert and

Howard. They looked at her expectantly, but she just sat there quietly, thinking hard.

'Well?' Howard said finally. 'What was that all about?'

'Something just happened there,' Sita said slowly. 'And I'm not entirely certain what.'

'What did he have to say?' said Rupert.

'Brian can't help us,' said Sita. 'I think he'd like to, but he's too frightened to go against Jones. And I mean *really* frightened.'

'Why?' said Rupert, shooting a quick glance in my direction. 'What's so special about Jones?'

'I don't know,' said Sita. 'Brian was too scared to say.'

'But he's a military policeman!' said Howard.

'Exactly,' said Sita. 'The kind of man who isn't easily intimidated. Which suggests there has to be a lot more to Jones than we're seeing.'

'I'm sorry,' said Rupert. 'But I'm not buying into any of this conspiracy stuff. Sir Dennis's important new appointment made him a target, that's all. We have to help Jones and Penny find the killer, if only because I won't feel safe until they do.'

'But I'm on to something here,' said Sita.

'No!' said Rupert. 'I may not be happy with the way Jones is doing things, but I don't see any reason why I should trust you more than him. You just want a story; Jones wants to catch a killer. We have to trust him.'

'He's right, Sita,' said Howard. 'If Jones is right, and someone in this carriage did murder Sir Dennis, how can we be sure you're not the killer, trying to turn us against the one man who might be able to prove that it's you?'

'I'm not a killer!' said Sita. 'I'm a journalist!'

'We have to trust Jones and Penny, because we can't trust any of us,' said Rupert. 'They're the only ones who can protect us from each other.'

He got up, returned to his seat and sat down with his back to them. Sita looked at Howard.

'Do you honestly think I could have killed Sir Dennis?'

'Don't get me wrong,' said Howard. 'I won't shed any tears over that man being dead. Whoever killed him did the world a favour. And you have given me something to think about.

Thank you for that. It helps take my mind off other things. But . . . I'm really not convinced by any of the things you've said. So you go right ahead and do whatever you feel you have to, but please leave me out of it.'

He got up and went back to his own seat. Sita glared after him, then at Rupert and finally at me and Penny. I saw no reason to look away this time, so I just smiled cheerfully back at her. Sita turned away and scowled at the empty seat before her. I could tell she was still working on some new form of rebellion, so after a moment's thought I got up, walked along the aisle and sat down opposite her. She looked up, startled.

'I'm not answering any more questions!'

'You know, you don't have to be afraid of me, Sita.'

'I'm not afraid of you!' she shot back immediately. 'Brian is the one who's scared of you, though God alone knows why. You're not exactly impressive. What did you do to Brian?'

'He wanted to know the truth about me,' I said. 'But when he got a glimpse of it, he couldn't cope.'

Sita frowned. 'Am I supposed to understand any of that?'

'Not really,' I said.

'Just as well, then.'

'I'm only interested in working out what happened to Sir Dennis,' I said patiently. 'Unless you're the killer, you have no reason to be afraid of me.'

'Do you think I did it?' said Sita, meeting my gaze unwaveringly.

'I'm so tired I don't know what to think,' I said.

She seemed a little surprised that I was ready to be so open with her. Or that I'd admit to something so ordinary as weariness.

'We're all tired,' she said finally. 'Comes from not being able to trust anyone.'

'I saw you talking with Rupert and Howard, and then Brian,' I said carefully.

She sniffed loudly. 'You've no reason to worry about any of them. They don't have enough balls between them to give you any trouble.'

'Unlike you?'

Sita smiled coldly. 'You're running out of time, aren't you?

And you're no closer to finding the killer than when you started. What will you do when we get to Bath and you have to admit to the authorities that you've got nothing? Are you going to have us all arrested?'

'I don't do things like that,' I said.

'Then what do you do?' said Sita. 'Who are you really, Mr Jones?'

'I'm the one who gets to the truth,' I said. 'Whatever it takes.'

'I thought that was my job,' said Sita. She sat back in her chair and folded her arms defiantly. 'What do you want from me?'

'Just some space. And a little cooperation,' I said. 'So I can do my job.'

'Don't let me stop you,' said Sita.

You just know some conversations aren't going to go anywhere you want them to. I went back to sit with Penny. She slipped her arm through mine and leaned against me companionably.

'I'm guessing that didn't go at all well.'

'Not really, no.'

'I could have told you that, darling. Did you really think you were going to get anything useful out of her?'

'No,' I said. 'But I had to try.'

Penny sighed. 'What are we going to do?'

'I'm thinking.'

'Well, think faster, darling.'

And then we both looked round as Rupert rose suddenly from his seat and hurried down the aisle to join Howard.

'What the hell is going on now?' I said quietly to Penny. 'Why can't everyone just stay put?'

'I'm glad someone's talking to Howard,' said Penny. 'He needs bringing out of himself.' She looked at me. 'Do you have to listen to them this time? It might not be anything to do with the murder.'

'I still need to know,' I said.

Howard was looking wearily and not at all patiently at Rupert. His voice was barely polite.

'What do you want now, Rupert? I've got a lot on my mind and I'm really not in the mood for company.'

'Can't honestly say that I am,' said Rupert. 'But there are things we need to talk about, Howard.'

'Like what?'

'Who do you think the killer is?'

'Why are you asking me?' said Howard. He actually sounded a little amused at the idea that he of all people might know the answer.

'Because I've decided that out of everyone in this carriage, you're the only one I trust,' said Rupert. 'Though, admittedly, that isn't saying much.'

'I'm flattered,' said Howard. 'I think. But I genuinely have no idea who killed Sir Dennis. It's all a complete mystery to me.'

'I know I'm not the killer,' said Rupert. 'And I really can't see you in the role either.'

'Why not?' said Howard, a little nettled at being dismissed so quickly. 'I might have it in me to kill a man like that.'

'I think you're only interested in killing one person,' said Rupert.

Howard sighed quietly. 'You heard me talking to Jones.'

'You did get a bit loud there, at the end,' said Rupert. 'I'm pretty sure everyone heard.'

'It's still no one's business but mine,' said Howard. 'Look, Rupert . . . I really don't care about the murder, or who might be involved in it.'

'But what if Jones is right, and the killer decides he needs to finish us all off before we get to Bath?'

'I'm not interested!'

Rupert sat back in his seat and studied Howard carefully. 'You know, you and I have a lot in common.'

Howard gave Rupert his full attention. 'All right, I didn't see that one coming. What could you and I possibly have in common?'

'You lost everything that mattered to you,' said Rupert. 'And I think I may be about to.'

Howard nodded slowly. 'What is it you want from me, Rupert?'

'I've got enough shit about to rain down on me,' said Rupert. 'I want this murder business over and done with, so I can concentrate on my own problems. I need you to help me figure out what's going on here.'

'The killer can't be one of us,' said Howard. 'We were all in plain sight when Sir Dennis died.'

'Jones seems pretty sure that one of us must have managed it somehow,' said Rupert.

'That's his problem.'

'Unfortunately,' said Rupert, 'he seems determined to make it *our* problem.'

Howard suddenly sat up straight as a new idea took hold of him. He looked quickly at me and then turned back to Rupert.

'What if the killer really isn't one of us? What if . . . it's him?'

'What?' said Rupert. 'I don't . . .' And then he stopped and looked quickly at me before staring wide-eyed at Howard. 'You think *Jones* killed Sir Dennis? How is that even possible?'

'Think about it,' said Howard, fixing Rupert with a hard stare. 'None of us left the compartment. But Jones did. We all saw him do it. And then he came back and told us Sir Dennis was dead.'

Rupert slumped in his seat as though he'd been hit. It was a while before he felt able to say anything.

'If you're right, then we've been trapped in here with the killer all along. It does make sense. What better cover could a professional killer have than to masquerade as the man investigating the murder? But then . . . that would have to mean Penny—'

'Yes,' said Howard. 'She'd have to be a part of it too.'

'But I like her!' said Rupert. 'She seems so nice, so helpful . . .'

'That's probably her job,' said Howard. 'To make us think someone was on our side and keep us from seeing the obvious.'

'But . . . What can we do?' said Rupert.

'There's only one thing you can do: challenge Jones to his face and, if need be, take him down.'

'What? Are you kidding?' Rupert's voice rose sharply, and it took him a moment to bring it back under control again. 'Why does it have to be me?'

'Because you're the brave young man, and I'm not.' Howard sighed. 'I'd rather not be involved in any of this, but I can see I'm never going to get a moment's peace until we sort it out. I can't go up against Jones, because he'd never take me seriously. And Brian is afraid of him. I suppose if you're not up to it, we could always ask Sita; I don't think she's afraid of anyone.'

'Of course not,' said Rupert. 'She takes on the establishment for fun. But I think . . . this is going to take all of us. You, me, Sita and Brian. It's not like Jones is going to admit anything, is he? But if we all just pile on to him and drag him down . . .'

'Oh, hell,' said Howard, smiling suddenly. 'Why not? It's something to do, until I get to Bath.'

They both got up out of their seats, carefully not looking in my direction, and walked casually over to join Sita. I kept watching and listening, fascinated to see how far this would go. Sita fixed Rupert and Howard with a cold stare as they sat down facing her.

'What do you two want? I thought you'd decided you didn't believe anything I had to say?'

'We think Jones is the killer,' said Rupert.

'We think it's a possibility,' Howard said quickly.

'It was your idea!' said Rupert.

'Keep your voice down,' said Howard.

A slow grin spread across Sita's face. 'OK . . . I like that. It would explain a lot. I never did trust the man.'

'Rupert thinks we need to overpower Jones, maybe tie him up, before we get to Bath,' said Howard.

'It was your idea to confront him!' said Rupert.

'But we're going to need Brian's help to take Jones down,' said Howard, concentrating on Sita. 'Do you think you could talk him into it?'

'I might be able to,' said Sita.

They all looked surreptitiously at me, while I pretended not to notice.

'Hold it,' said Rupert. 'Jones has a gun. He took it from Brian, remember? If he even suspected we were on to him . . . Maybe we'd be better off waiting till we get to Bath, and then denounce him to the authorities there. Let them handle him.'

'Why would they take our word for it?' said Howard. 'He's one of them.'

'Only if he is who he says he is,' said Sita. 'Maybe he killed the real security man and took his place!'

'I don't think we can wait till we get to Bath,' said Rupert, changing direction at speed. 'Remember what Jones said earlier, about the murderer needing to kill all the witnesses?'

'I think if Jones was going to do that, he'd already have done it,' said Howard.

'He could be waiting for just the right moment,' Rupert said stubbornly.

'We've got to get that gun away from him,' said Sita.

'How?' said Rupert. 'Professional assassins are probably very good at spotting people who want to take their guns away from them.'

'You two distract him,' said Howard. 'And I'll move in from behind and take the gun out of his pocket.'

'Why you?' said Sita.

'Because Howard doesn't care what happens to him,' said Rupert.

Sita looked at Howard. 'That's no way to live.'

'That's what I thought,' said Howard.

Sita frowned. 'If we're going to take Jones down, we're going to need a better plan than just sneaking the gun out of his pocket. Whatever Jones might really be, he's definitely a professional. You'd never get anywhere near him.'

'And even if he didn't suspect something, Penny probably would,' said Rupert. 'She doesn't miss much.'

'Then someone will just have to talk to Penny,' said Howard. 'Keep her distracted.'

'You should do it,' Rupert said to Sita. 'Girl to girl, that sort of thing . . .'

She shook her head immediately. 'No offence, but I'm a better fighter than both of you put together. You can't do this without me. You talk to her, Rupert.'

'Why me?'

'Because she wouldn't see you as a threat.'

'She has a point,' said Howard.

Rupert nodded glumly. 'All right. I'll think of something to say . . .'

Howard looked thoughtfully at Sita. 'So it's you and me against the experienced security man. How are we going to do this, exactly?'

Sita smiled. 'We use an old street tactic, from my student protest days. How to stop a policeman, without being violent: send a pretty girl to hug him tightly. Before Jones figures out how to react, you get the gun out of his pocket and then pass it to me.'

'Why should you have it?' said Howard.

'Do you know anything about guns?' said Sita.

'No. Do you?'

'Enough to fake it.'

Howard shook his head. 'I'm not sure about this . . . You said it yourself: Jones is a professional. You saw how easily he disarmed Brian and took down the private detective.'

'Are you scared of him?' said Sita.

'Yes!' said Howard. 'There's something about that man . . .'

'He's just putting on an act, to intimidate us into behaving,' said Sita. 'He's not really scary, any more than Penny is really friendly.'

'Bad cop, good cop,' said Howard.

'Exactly,' said Sita.

'He could still be dangerous,' said Rupert.

'No! Hold it! Wait a minute . . .' Sita frowned fiercely, concentrating, and then shook her head regretfully. 'No. Nice try, boys, but . . . no. Forget it. Jones isn't the killer.'

'What?' said Rupert. 'Why not? How can you be so sure?'

'Because if he had been the killer, he wouldn't have put so much time and effort into trying to get a confession out of one of us,' said Sita. 'And there was already a railway guard outside the locked toilet, before Jones got there. I heard him banging on the door and calling out. So Sir Dennis must have been dead before Jones left the carriage.'

'Oh, hell!' said Rupert. 'I really thought I was on to something there.'

They all sat and looked at each other for a long moment.

'Well,' said Howard. 'That was a nice touch of excitement, but I think I'll go back to my own seat now. I have some important brooding to be getting on with.'

'Isn't there anything we can do to help?' said Rupert.

'No,' said Howard.

He went back to his seat. Rupert and Sita watched him go.

'You can't help someone who doesn't want to be helped,' said Sita.

'Maybe we could help him to want that,' said Rupert.

'He's had a long time to think about this,' said Sita. 'What could we possibly say to Howard that he hasn't already come up with himself?'

Rupert didn't have an answer to that. He went back to his own seat, and Sita went back to concentrating on her own thoughts. I was quietly relieved that what could have been an open rebellion had come to nothing before I had to do something to defuse it. And yet . . . After listening to all of that, I was more convinced than ever that none of them could be the murderer. Which put me right back where I started.

Penny suddenly grabbed my arm and squeezed it hard. 'Ishmael! I've just had an idea!'

'Oh, good,' I said. 'That's one more than me.'

'Maybe there's a reason why we never saw anyone go past us! What if the killer released a gas into the carriage that put all of us to sleep? Just long enough for him to get past us, kill Sir Dennis and then hurry back to his seat before any of us woke up? We wouldn't know anything had happened!'

I looked at her.

'And that's your idea?'

'Yes! What do you think?'

'I think you've been watching too much television,' I said.

'But it would explain the gap in our memories . . .'

'It wouldn't explain how the killer was able to smuggle a canister of gas into the compartment without being noticed, and then hide the empty canister afterwards. Or how he could time the effects so exactly, when any gas affects different people differently. Or a dozen other practical problems. No, Penny, that kind of thing only works in bad television shows. There's a reason why they call them mission impossible. And, anyway, if there had been a gas, I'd have smelt it.'

'All right!' said Penny. 'You come up with something!'

'I've been trying,' I said. 'And I've got nothing. I don't see how anyone could have done it.'

SIX

A Shot in the Dark

For a long moment, Penny and I just sat and stared at each other, both hoping the other would come up with something . . . but neither of us had anything to offer. Finally, Penny fixed me with her best stern stare.

'I've never known you to give up on a case before, Ishmael.'

'I'm not giving up,' I said. 'I'm just lost for where to go next.'

'We have to do something!' said Penny. 'We'll be arriving in Bath in . . .'

'Don't look at your watch!' I said sharply. 'The last thing we need right now is more pressure.'

'If we're stumped,' Penny said carefully, 'it can only be because we've missed something. Some vital clue, or piece of evidence, that would make everything fall into place. That's usually what happens at the end of one of our cases . . . Someone says something, or you spot something – and, just like that, you see everything in a new light. Then you put it all together and point out the murderer. So stop and think, Ishmael. What is it you're not seeing?'

I nodded slowly. 'When in doubt . . . assume that everyone has lied to you, and you can't trust anyone or anything to be what they seem to be.'

'All right,' Penny said steadily. 'Let's say we assume that's the case. Where does that take us?'

'It means we need to verify for ourselves that everything we think is true really is,' I said. 'Until we come up with something that clashes with what we've been told, and that's our new starting point.'

'Ishmael, we don't have time to check everything!'

'Then we check what we can,' I said. 'Starting with the darkened carriage.'

Penny frowned. 'Why there? I mean, we already know it's completely deserted.'

'We start with the next carriage because it's the only thing that stands between us and the rest of the train,' I said. 'If anything about that isn't what we've been told, then all our previous ideas fall apart.'

And, I thought but didn't say, *because I'm damned if I can think of anything else to do.*

I got to my feet and headed for the door, and Penny followed along behind me, saying nothing, just trusting me to know what I was doing. I admired her faith. I only wished I shared it. I was having trouble convincing myself I wasn't simply going through the motions, to make myself feel as if I was doing something. But since I would rather die than let Penny down, or let a murderer get away with killing someone right under my nose, I had no choice but to keep hammering away at the problem until either it broke or I did.

Brian looked at me sourly as I came down the aisle, and made no move to get out of the way. I stopped before him, and Penny was quickly there at my side.

'You should have let me run this investigation,' Brian said flatly. 'I'd have got the truth out of someone by now.'

'You might have intimidated a confession out of someone,' I said. 'But that's not the same thing.'

'It's better than nothing,' said Brian. 'Which is what you've got.'

'My investigation isn't over yet,' I said. 'You keep an eye on the passengers, while Penny and I check out the next carriage.'

Brian glanced back over his shoulder. 'There's no one in there; I'd have noticed.'

'I never said there was,' I said calmly.

'Then what do you expect to find, in an empty carriage?'

'Something I didn't see the last time I looked,' I said, doing my best to sound confident.

Brian sniffed and shrugged. 'Go ahead. Knock your-selves out. You're the ones who'll have to explain to the authorities in Bath why you haven't arrested anyone for Sir Dennis's murder.'

I let that one go, as though I hadn't even felt the breeze of its passing. 'Try not to let anyone get up to anything while we're gone.'

'But don't break them,' Penny said firmly. 'Play nicely, Brian. Innocent until proven guilty, remember?'

He smiled briefly. 'You were never in the army.' The smile disappeared as he shot me a hard look. 'I want my gun back.'

I had to raise an eyebrow. 'You think you're going to need a gun to cope with two businessmen and a reporter?'

'It's my gun,' said Brian.

'You can have it back when we get to Bath,' I said. 'If you've been good.'

I looked at him steadily until he lowered his eyes and stepped aside. This whole alpha-male routine was getting very old, but it appeared to be the only thing he knew how to respond to. I brushed past Brian, and the door hissed open. I stepped out into the vestibule, and Penny hurried through to join me. The door closed behind us, and she let out a sigh of relief.

'Damn, I'm glad to be out of there. The atmosphere was getting so thick you could slice it up and hand it round on a plate.' She looked at me. 'Do you still see Brian as a suspect? Is that why you don't want to give him back his gun?'

'I'm not putting a weapon in that man's hand as long as I'm trapped in the same carriage as him,' I said firmly. 'Brian has the unmistakable air of someone who's been trained to shoot first and let someone else ask the questions afterwards.'

I looked around the vestibule. It was brightly lit, completely empty and very quiet. Penny walked over to stand before the toilet cubicle. I moved in beside her.

'What is it?'

'When you said *doubt everything*,' she said slowly, 'did you consider the possibility that Sir Dennis might not actually be in there?'

I looked at her. 'You think he might have got up from his throne and gone for a little walk?'

'Wouldn't be the first time on one of our cases,' said Penny.

I tried the door. 'It's still locked. And Sir Dennis was quite definitely dead, the last time I looked.'

'I refer you to my previous comment,' said Penny. 'But even if he is one hundred per cent deceased and not at all in the mood for a stroll, someone might still have removed the body. If our killer was able to break into a locked cubicle to attack him, why couldn't they do it again to get at the body?'

'Why would they want to?' I said.

'To make the body disappear?' said Penny. 'It wouldn't do much for our credibility, would it, if we opened the toilet door when we arrived in Bath and there was no one in there? And it's always possible there's some evidence on the body that would incriminate the killer.'

I shook my head. 'We can't open the door without the guard's remote control device. And I really don't want to have to search the whole train for Mr Holder if he isn't where he's supposed to be.'

'We could always send Brian to go fetch him,' said Penny. 'Having something useful to do might calm him down a bit.'

'But then who'd watch the passengers in First Class?' I said.

'You really think they need watching?'

'They're still the only real suspects we've got,' I said. I turned away from the toilet and gave the door to the darkened carriage my full attention. 'Unless we can find something useful in there.'

'Why don't you just break into the toilet?' said Penny.

'Because then I'd have to explain how,' I said. 'No normal human would be strong enough.'

I broke off as a thought occurred to me, and I turned back to the cubicle, leaned in close and pressed my cheek flat against the door.

'Ishmael?' said Penny. 'What are you doing?'

I inhaled deeply and then straightened up again and stepped back.

'He's in there. I can smell the body through the crack in the door.'

'Oh, ick,' said Penny.

I moved over to the door to the next carriage and peered through the glass partition. Penny crowded in beside me.

'Can't see a damned thing,' she said after a moment. 'It's completely dark.'

'I can see enough to be sure that no one's home,' I said.

'So nothing's changed.'

'Not necessarily,' I said. 'The last time I was in there, I didn't take the time to search the carriage properly. I didn't see the point then.'

'You really think we need to go in there?' said Penny.

I looked at Penny, careful to keep all traces of amusement out of my face and my voice. 'Trust me: there are no rogue psychics, professional assassins or any kind of bogeyman hiding in this compartment.'

'So what's the point of going in there?' said Penny.

'To search for any evidence I might have missed the first time,' I said patiently. 'If, by any chance, it turns out that I am wrong, and something unpleasant should come looming up out of the dark, you have my full permission to punch it in the face.'

'That would make me feel better,' said Penny. 'What sort of evidence are we looking for? I mean, Sir Dennis was killed in the toilet.'

'I don't know,' I said. 'I just can't shake this feeling that I've overlooked something. Think about it: this is the only carriage on the entire train where the lights failed. There must be a reason for that, and the most obvious one I can think of is to hide something important from me.'

'That's a bit of a stretch, darling,' Penny said tactfully.

'It's a hell of a reach,' I said. 'But it's all we've got.'

'All right!' said Penny. 'This is a wonderful theory, and I am all for it! Let us proceed immediately into the dark and spooky deserted carriage and investigate the shit out of it. I will be right behind you, ready to punch out anything that moves.'

'I love it when you have such faith in me,' I said.

I stepped forward and the door hissed open. And then I stopped to consider that. Penny made a startled noise as she bumped into me from behind.

'Give me some warning, Ishmael! Why have we stopped?'

'I'm just wondering why this door is still working,' I said, 'when there's no power in the carriage?'

'I don't know,' said Penny. 'Because the door's on a separate circuit?'

'Ah,' I said. 'Yes, that would do it. Sorry. For a moment there, I was sure I was on to something.'

I entered the carriage. The light spilling in behind me was only just enough to illuminate the nearest seats. Beyond that I could make out basic shapes, but no details. I looked around slowly, checking for anything that seemed out of place.

'I still can't see anything,' Penny murmured from just behind my shoulder. 'Shouldn't the emergency lights be working at least, to point out to passengers where the exits are?'

'The whole system must be down,' I said. 'Which, of course, isn't in any way suspicious.'

'You have eyes like a hawk,' said Penny. 'Or an owl. Is anything standing out to you?'

'No,' I said. 'I'm not seeing, hearing or even smelling anything out of the ordinary.'

'I still think I'll stay behind you,' said Penny. 'I've always found you make an excellent human shield in times of danger. For someone who isn't actually human. I am still ready to throw a punch over your shoulder, if need be.'

'Why are you so obsessed with hitting someone?'

Penny sniffed loudly. 'Doesn't this entire case make you feel like punching somebody really hard?'

'You may have a point there.'

I slowly made my way down the aisle, out of the light and into the dark, bracing myself against the rocking of the train. I carefully studied each row of seats I passed, straining my eyes against the gloom. Behind me, I could hear Penny bumping into practically everything, as she did her best to follow me down the aisle. I'd given her eyes time to adjust, but there wasn't enough light in the carriage for human eyes to work with. She stopped suddenly and called after me.

'This is useless, Ishmael! I can't even see you, never mind what you're doing.'

'Then go back and guard the door,' I said, not glancing

back over my shoulder in case it broke my concentration. 'Make sure no one gets past you, from either direction.'

'I can do that,' said Penny. I heard her bump and thud her way back to the door, and then her quiet sigh of relief once she was safely back in the light. 'OK . . . I'm looking into the vestibule, and no one's followed us here from First Class.'

'Is Brian watching us?'

'No. I can see his back through the glass partition.'

'Good. Keep an eye on him.'

'There is a definite limit to how many directions I can look in at once, darling.'

'Well . . . do your best.'

I carried on down the aisle, a few steps at a time, and then stopped abruptly. There was something blocking the aisle, right up by the end door. I moved forward cautiously until I was close enough to recognize the obstruction as the private detective Dee's trolley. The one she'd had such trouble controlling in her role as a tea lady. It was standing alone and abandoned, with no sign of Dee anywhere. I checked the trolley carefully, but there was nothing about it to suggest what might have happened to Dee. No sign of a struggle anywhere around it, and no drops of blood on the trolley itself.

It was always possible Dee had just abandoned it, along with her role as tea lady, now her true identity had been established, but I didn't think so. I just knew something bad had happened to her.

I called quietly back to Penny, filling her in on what I'd found, and then I eased past the trolley and stood before the end door. I knocked loudly and called out to Eric. He opened the door immediately, and light spilled in from the vestibule. He looked at me enquiringly.

'What is it, sir? Has something happened?'

'Did Dee go past you when she came back this way?' I said bluntly.

'No, sir,' said Eric. 'I haven't seen her since she insisted on going back to First Class. Sorry about that, sir. I know I shouldn't have talked to her, but . . .'

'I understand,' I said. 'She was a very forceful lady.'

'That she was, sir.'

'Are you sure she couldn't have got past you, without you seeing?'

'No, sir. I've been here all this time, guarding the door. I was starting to get worried that I hadn't seen her for a while.'

'Lock this door again,' I said. 'And whatever happens, don't leave the vestibule unless I tell you otherwise.'

'Of course, sir.'

He closed the door, and I waited till I heard the lock turn. I looked at the trolley again. It proved Dee had got this far at least, but how could she have vanished between First Class and the railway guard's vestibule? There was no way out of the darkened carriage; the only doors were in the two vestibules.

I was sure there was no body hidden anywhere in the darkened carriage. Could the murderer have killed Dee and then stuffed her body in the First-Class toilet cubicle, along with Sir Dennis? No, I would have picked up her scent when I smelled Sir Dennis. So what did that leave?

I smiled suddenly in the dark and got down on all fours. I ran my hands over the thinly carpeted floor, pressing my fingertips into the fibres. I couldn't feel anything unusual – no tears or rumpling or anything to indicate a struggle had taken place.

I moved carefully along on my hands and knees, heading back toward the door, checking the ground I'd already walked because I couldn't afford to miss anything. And finally I caught a faint whiff of something. I pushed my face right down over the carpet, and the smell grew stronger. I breathed in deeply and the scents of a recent murder filled my head. The piss and shit the body always lets go at time of death, as the sphincters give up. Things that would have been retained inside Sir Dennis's clothes, which is why the scents were so faint I missed them the first time around. Anywhere else they would have dissipated by now, but they'd been preserved by the still air and the contained environment. My first real clue – and just like that, I knew exactly what had happened to Sir Dennis.

'Ishmael?' said Penny. 'You've been quiet a really long time, and I can't see you anywhere. Are you all right?'

'Fine,' I said happily. 'Just fine.'

I rose to my feet, suppressed the urge to do a little jig of triumph – because I am, after all, a professional – and went back to join Penny. I told her what I'd found and started to go into details, but she shook her head firmly.

'Ick. And I mean serious ick. Are you sure?'

'Some scents are always going to be immediately identifiable,' I said. 'You're welcome to go and smell them yourself.'

'I am entirely ready to take your word for it,' said Penny. 'Tell me you didn't get any of it on your clothes.'

'There are no actual stains as such; it was all . . .'

'Not listening! Hands over ears, not listening.'

'But don't you see what this means?' I said. 'This proves Sir Dennis didn't die inside the toilet. He was killed right here, in this compartment. When he left First Class and stepped out into the vestibule, someone must have been waiting for him. Perhaps they called to him from the dark and asked for his help, to lure him in. Sir Dennis was murdered here, his body fell to the floor, and then the murderer carried the body to the toilet and arranged Sir Dennis in position, to make it look as if he'd been caught by surprise.'

'To conceal where and when he was killed!' said Penny.

'All of which means we know who did it,' I said happily.

Penny looked at me. 'We do?'

'Of course,' I said. 'There's only one person on this train who could have done it.'

'You see?' said Penny. 'All it takes is one new clue, one new insight, and you're a murder-solving machine! So who is it?'

I looked behind me. 'Hush . . .'

Penny moved in close beside me and lowered her voice to a whisper.

'What is it?'

'I just heard the far door open,' I said quietly. 'Someone has entered this carriage from the other end.'

'But that door is supposed to be locked and guarded!'

'I know,' I said. 'Now stand quietly and wait for them to come to us.'

I watched the dark figure make his way down the aisle. He

moved easily and confidently, as though he could see as clearly in the dark as me. Penny gripped my arm tightly as she listened to the approaching footsteps. And then the figure stopped just short of us and turned on a flashlight. Penny cried out despite herself, blinded by the sudden glare, but I just narrowed my eyes and stared back into it.

'Hello, Eric,' I said to the railway guard. 'Why have you left your post, after I just ordered you not to?'

'Oh! You did give me shock, sir!' said Eric, quickly lowering his flashlight and turning it off. 'I didn't expect you to still be here. And you, of course, miss.'

Penny let out a sigh of relief, let go of my arm and glared at Eric. 'You must have seen us here; why didn't you announce yourself?'

'I'm really very sorry, miss,' said Eric. 'But I wasn't sure who you were. I just thought I heard some movement in here, and since I thought Mr Jones would be gone by now, and no one is supposed to be in this carriage, I thought I'd better check it out. I hope you'll pardon me for being a little overcautious, but with a murderer loose somewhere on the train . . .'

'Quite understandable, Eric,' I said. 'But why didn't you use your flashlight till you were right on top of us?'

'Didn't think of it, sir. I've been walking up and down these carriages for so many years I could do it with my eyes shut.' Eric shifted his feet uncomfortably. 'And, of course, if you were someone I didn't want to meet, the sudden light was the only weapon I had. If you could tell I was coming, sir, why didn't you say anything?'

'I was pretty sure it was you,' I said. 'Because you're the only one who could have unlocked the far door. But I thought I'd better wait before I said anything, just in case you turned out to be somebody I didn't want to meet. After all, if another person could get through the locked door . . .'

'Of course, sir,' Eric said quickly. 'I could have been the killer! But I've been working in the far vestibule all this time and I haven't seen anyone.'

'Still no luck restoring the lights?' Penny asked kindly.

'Not a bit, miss,' said Eric. 'We'll have to wait for the engineers to take a look, once we get to Bath.'

'Any idea why the lights only went out in this particular carriage?' I said.

'I wouldn't know, sir. I've checked all the other carriages, and they're fine.' He hesitated, choosing his words carefully. 'Can I just ask, sir, what are you and the young lady doing in here?'

'Looking for clues,' I said. 'It's what we do.'

'Of course, sir. Very persevering of you. Did you find any?'

'I found something,' I said. 'You'd better join the rest of us in First Class, Eric. I may need your assistance.'

'I really shouldn't, sir,' Eric said dubiously. 'I have my other passengers to think of. I mean, what if the lights should happen to fail in another carriage? People could hurt themselves in the dark.'

'If any of the other lights were going to fail, I think they would have done so by now,' I said. 'I need you with me, Eric, because I'm about to inform the First-Class passengers what really happened to Sir Dennis. I think you should be there to hear that, as a representative of the railway company. And to back me up, if it should prove necessary to restrain someone.'

Eric drew himself up. 'Of course, sir. You can depend on me. But are you sure, sir? I thought we knew how the gentleman died?'

'No,' I said. 'We only thought we did.'

I led the way out of the darkened carriage. Penny hurried after me, and Eric brought up the rear. I paused for a moment in the vestibule, so that Penny and Eric's eyes could adjust to the light. Eric gestured at the toilet cubicle.

'Do you need me to open that up again, sir?'

'I don't think so,' I said. 'Do you still have your remote control?'

'Of course, sir. Never without it.' He smiled and patted one of his jacket pockets in a self-important way. 'All part of my duties; you never know when it might be needed.'

'That's what I thought,' I said.

I went back into First Class, and the first thing I noticed was that Brian wasn't standing guard at the door. I looked down the compartment and there he was, wrestling with Sita.

They were rolling back and forth in the middle of the aisle, both of them putting up a fierce fight. I sighed and cleared my throat loudly. Brian and Sita broke off from what they were doing, looked back and saw me standing there. They both froze where they were.

'What is going on?' I said.

'Oh, let them play,' said Penny.

I looked at her. 'Am I missing something here?'

'Not for the first time,' said Penny. 'Those two have been trying to impress each other for ages. It's all part of fancying someone.'

Brian pushed Sita away from him, and they both scrambled to their feet and glared at each other.

'I do not fancy him!' Sita said loudly.

'I was just doing my duty!' said Brian, equally loudly.

'What happened?' I said, keeping my voice carefully neutral.

'She got Howard to distract me,' Brian said quickly. 'By saying he'd seen something out the window. When I went to look, she went after her laptop. Thought she could sneak it back to her seat without me noticing. But I didn't trust anyone here, so I kept an eye on her and caught her at it. She got her laptop down from the luggage rack, and when I took it off her, she attacked me.'

'He threw it on the floor!' said Sita.

'I thought I told you children to play nicely,' I said and then looked thoughtfully at Sita. 'Why did you want your laptop so badly? We'll be in Bath soon.'

'I wanted to get the story to my editor before then,' said Sita. 'I don't trust you or your people not to slap a D-notice on the whole thing and shut me out. I know how this works!'

'You don't have the whole story yet,' I said. 'I'm about to tell it to you. Now pick up your laptop – and behave.'

Sita knelt down, grabbed hold of her laptop and then stood up, clutching it to her protectively. I smiled calmly back at her.

'Please find a seat, Sita. You too, Brian. Rupert, Howard, pay attention, please. It's time for me to explain the exact circumstances leading up to Sir Dennis's death. Which aren't at all what you think they are.'

Sita stared at me for a moment, shocked into silence, and

then dropped into the nearest seat. Brian sat down next to her. Howard and Rupert turned completely around in their seats, so they could get a better look at me. Everyone seemed startled, caught off guard, but none of them said anything. I nodded to Eric.

'You can sit down too.'

'It's really not my place, sir . . .'

'I won't tell anyone if you won't.'

I gestured for him to go and sit with the others, and he did so reluctantly. I looked at Penny and gestured for her to go back and stand by the door. Just in case. She nodded quickly and took up her position.

I stood easily in the middle of the aisle, looking from face to face, taking my time. Everyone seemed very eager to hear what I was going to say, and I had to struggle to hold back a satisfied smile. It had been a long hard slog to get to where I was now, and I felt I'd earned the right to make the most of it.

'Do you know who did it?' Howard said abruptly. 'Do you know who killed Sir Dennis?'

'Is it one of us, after all?' said Rupert.

'It can't be!' Sita said stubbornly.

'Let me run you through the sequence of events,' I said, refusing to be hurried. 'Sir Dennis left this carriage to visit the toilet, after ordering his bodyguard not to accompany him. This was what the killer had been waiting for: his first break. He'd probably have found some way to separate Sir Dennis from his bodyguard, but when presented with such a perfect opportunity, he ran with it.

'So Sir Dennis went out into the vestibule, but before he could use the toilet, someone called out to him. A person Sir Dennis had no reason to suspect, let alone fear. This person lured Sir Dennis into the darkened carriage on some pretext and then attacked and murdered him. Afterwards, the killer arranged the body on the toilet to make it look as if he'd been surprised there.'

I paused for a moment, so they could all consider the implications. They took it in turns to glance at each other, surprised by this sudden change in what they thought had happened, but none of them said anything. They just turned back and looked at me steadily, waiting for me to continue.

'Of course,' I said, 'none of that helped with the main problem: how to identify the murderer. Given that the next carriage along was locked and guarded, cutting us off from the rest of the train, it was obvious that only the people travelling in this carriage were viable suspects. But how could anyone from First Class have got past Penny and me to get to Sir Dennis, without either of us seeing them? The simple answer is that they couldn't have. The murderer never was any of the people in this compartment.'

It took a moment, and then Rupert and Howard, Sita and Brian suddenly all looked extremely relieved as they realized they were no longer suspects. They made a variety of pleased and happy noises, and then started to babble, their voices rising as they threw questions at me. I raised a hand and they immediately stopped talking. If there was more, they wanted to hear it. I smiled. It felt good to be on top of the situation at last.

'I forgot, for a while, the first rule of investigating murders. Trust nobody and assume everyone is lying to you. Which is, of course, what happened here. You all had secrets that you were ready to lie about to conceal the truth from me, but they all emerged during questioning, and none of them appeared to have anything to do with the murder. So if none of you had the motive, means or opportunity to be the killer, what did that leave? It took me a while to remember that all of my reasoning was based on the belief that the next carriage along was completely impassable. I think I accepted that so quickly because I wanted to believe it, because it made my job so much easier if I didn't have to suspect and question everyone on the train.

'I'd been told the far door to the next carriage was locked and guarded. But I didn't know that for a fact. I only believed it to be true because the railway guard told me it was. A man in a uniform, whom everyone is used to accepting as an authority figure. But if no one in this carriage could possibly be the killer, then that meant the killer must have come from the other end of the train. Which, in turn, had to mean that the far door wasn't locked. So the guard must have lied to me.'

I turned to face the railway guard. 'And why would you do that, Eric? Because you're the murderer. You killed Sir Dennis in the darkened carriage and then dumped him in the toilet to confuse things.'

Everyone turned quickly to look at Eric, who stared blankly back at them. Brian started to rise up out of his seat, but I gestured sharply for him to stay put. He sank back, scowling.

'Not yet, Brian,' I said. 'I haven't finished with Eric yet.'

'What are you talking about?' said Eric. He sounded honestly outraged. 'I'm not a killer. I'm the train guard.'

'And the next best thing to an invisible man,' I said. 'Someone we all take for granted, someone that no one ever challenges, who can turn up anywhere, for any reason. An authority figure on the train, whose word everyone just tends to accept. Hard even to remember, because most people only see the uniform and the function, not the man himself. Which is, of course, what made it so easy for you to kill Sir Dennis. He would never have seen a mere functionary as a threat, not to someone as important as him.'

Eric jumped to his feet and glared hotly around the compartment before settling on me again.

'You can't label me a killer, just because you haven't come up with anyone else to blame!'

'You put a lot of effort into misleading me,' I said calmly. 'But once I realized it had to be you, a whole bunch of small but significant facts started dropping into place.'

'This is insane . . .' said Eric. 'You have no proof I'm involved in any of this!'

'I found evidence of Sir Dennis's death in the next carriage,' I said. 'From where the body had been lying on the floor.' I didn't go into details; they didn't need to know. 'In the end, though, you supplied the main clue yourself, Eric. You used your remote control to unlock the toilet door from the outside. A device you told me could override any electronic system on the train. You were the only person who could have locked the toilet door from the outside, after Sir

Dennis had been placed there, making it look as though he'd locked it himself from the inside. And you were the only one who could turn off the lights in just the one carriage and make sure they stayed off. I don't know why it took me so long to realize all of this. In my defence, I can only say there have been a great many complications and distractions in this case. Not least because you made me waste so much time questioning people who couldn't possibly have been the murderer.'

I stopped for a moment to look politely at Eric, but he just stood where he was, saying nothing. So I carried on.

'I don't see how this could have been a personal killing for you, so it must have been a professional hit. No doubt the authorities in Bath will discover who you're working for. All I have to do is hold on to you until then.'

Eric pulled a gun from inside his jacket and pointed it at me, smiling coldly. I stood very still.

'All right,' I said, 'I didn't see that one coming.'

The three passengers made loud startled noises, and Brian stirred ominously in his seat. Eric waved his gun back and forth, threatening everyone.

'Shut up!' he said loudly. 'Everyone stay where they are! I'll shoot the first one to get out of their seat!'

The three passengers stayed right where they were. Brian subsided reluctantly. I was a little relieved about that. I could see all kinds of things that could go wrong if Brian was to get involved with a desperate man holding a gun. I took a step forward, to attract Eric's attention, and he immediately trained his gun on me again. I gave him my best reassuring smile.

'Take it easy, Eric. There's no need for any unpleasantness. Though I have to ask: if you had a gun all along, why didn't you just shoot Sir Dennis?'

'Shut up!' said Eric. 'You don't know everything. I had my reasons.'

He backed down the aisle to the other end of the compartment, to make it easier for him to cover everyone. It was obvious from the way Eric was holding the gun that he didn't have much experience with firearms. If anything, that made him even more dangerous. An amateur is always going to be more likely to do something unnecessary.

I glanced quickly around the carriage to make sure no one was planning anything heroic. Rupert and Howard seemed properly intimidated, sinking well down in their seats to make themselves less obvious targets. Sita seemed fascinated by everything that was happening, and not nearly scared enough for her own safety, but at least she wasn't doing anything to attract attention to herself. I wouldn't have been surprised if she started taking notes. And then I saw Brian gathering his legs under him, getting ready to jump up out of his seat.

'Stay where you are, Brian!' I said. 'That's an order.'

He glowered at me but stayed put. He still didn't look nearly impressed enough by the danger of the situation, so I glared at him.

'I just saved your life, Brian. He would have shot you down long before you could do anything.'

'You don't know that,' he said. 'I might have got lucky.'

'No one's that lucky,' I said.

'Someone has to do something!' Brian said loudly.

'I am doing something,' I said. 'I'm talking to the man.'

And then I realized Eric wasn't looking at me any more. He'd remembered Penny was standing guard at the other door. Eric smiled and aimed his gun at her.

'You. Get over here. Now!'

Penny looked at me, and I nodded quickly for her to do as he said. Eric looked rattled enough to shoot her as an example. Penny walked slowly down the aisle, not looking at me or the passengers. Eric waited till she was within reach and then grabbed hold of her, turned her around and pressed his gun against the side of her head.

'Don't move, girl, or I'll kill you. I mean it!'

'I believe you,' Penny said steadily.

'Take it easy, Eric,' I said, working hard on making my voice sound calm and reassuring. 'You have a hostage now, and that puts you in charge. So take your time and think about what you're going to do next.'

Eric looked quickly around the carriage. 'Does anyone else

have a gun? What about you, Bodyguard? Or you, Mr Jones? And don't lie! I'll know!'

'I have a gun,' I said steadily. 'I took it off the bodyguard earlier.'

'Take out your gun, Mr Jones,' said Eric, smiling coldly. 'Do it slowly and very carefully, and then drop it on the floor. Do it!'

I removed the gun from my jacket pocket, using just my thumb and forefinger, and dropped it on the floor at my feet.

'Now kick it away from you,' said Eric.

I did so, with just enough force that it disappeared under the nearest seat. Out of sight, but not out of mind if I saw a chance to go for it later.

'Anyone else?' said Eric, glaring around the carriage.

'Brian has a backup weapon,' I said. 'A second gun, in a concealed ankle holster.'

Brian looked at me, torn between outrage that I'd given his secret away and astonishment that I even knew about it.

'Give it up, Brian,' I said. 'We can't do anything while Eric has a gun at Penny's head.'

For a moment, I wondered whether Brian might do something reckless, but he just made a disgusted sound, drew his gun slowly and then threw it away. I nodded my thanks and then looked back at the guard.

'What now, Eric?' I said. 'You've got the only gun, and we're all helpless. But are you really planning to hold us all hostage until we get to Bath, where you must know the authorities will be waiting? What will you do then? Ask for a hostage negotiator, and hope that whatever package deal you can make won't include a hidden marksman?'

'Shut up!' said Eric. 'I'm thinking.'

'Don't back him into a corner, Ishmael,' murmured Penny.

'You could always pull the communication cord, Eric,' I said steadily. 'Wait for the train to stop, open an exterior door with your remote control, and then jump out and disappear into the countryside. But the driver has strict instructions not to stop for anything, hasn't he? And if you do pull the cord, the driver will know there's an emergency on the train, and he'll warn the authorities.'

'Shut up!' said Eric. 'Or I'll kill the girl!'

He pressed his gun against Penny's temple, hard enough to make her wince.

'I'm pretty sure he means it, Ishmael,' she said steadily.

'I'm just trying to make your situation clear, Eric,' I said quickly. 'You've got the gun, but there's nowhere you can go. Your best bet is to make a deal with me, now, before things get out of hand.'

'I'm in control here,' said Eric.

'For the moment,' I said. 'You don't come across as a professional assassin, Eric, so I'm guessing you were hired just because you were going to be on this train. I'm also guessing the whole thing was arranged in something of a hurry, because this was your employers' only opportunity to get to Sir Dennis before he took up his new position. But I have to ask, Eric: why did you break Sir Dennis's neck? That was so obviously foul play. If you didn't want to shoot him, why not try to make it look like an accident?'

'That was the plan,' said Eric. 'But the little shit wouldn't cooperate.'

He knew he shouldn't be talking to me, but he couldn't stop himself. He needed to explain to someone how clever he'd been, and how close he'd come to getting away with it. I encouraged him with steady eye contact and lots of nodding, to keep him talking. I wanted him focused on me and not on the gun at Penny's head.

'My employers wanted me to make it look like some kind of accident,' said Eric. 'Because that would be so much more humiliating than a murder. It would suit their purposes, they said, to make Sir Dennis look so dumb he didn't even last long enough to take up his new position. And then the men who chose him for the job would look even more stupid. My employers only had this one chance to get to Sir Dennis before he disappeared behind proper levels of protection, so they gave me the job and half the money in advance, and left it all up to me.

'You think you're so smart, everything worked out . . . You got some of it right, but did you really think we'd leave it to chance, as to whether Sir Dennis would need to use the toilet before we got to Bath? No, my employers used one of their psychics to subtly influence a very minor security person. Just enough to have him slip a little something into Sir Dennis's drink. So all I had to do was shut down the lights in the next carriage, kick all the people out and wait. The plan was to lure him into the dark, slam his head against something hard, make sure he was dead and then raise the alarm. It would look like he'd tripped and hurt himself, because he was stupid enough to wander around in the dark on his own. Trust me, people do dumber things on trains all the time. And no one would ever suspect I had anything to do with it! Why would they? I'm just a railway guard.

'My employers only gave me this gun because I insisted on it. I needed to be sure I could protect myself if anything went wrong. I was getting ready to throw it away – we were getting close to Bath and I couldn't afford for anyone to find it on me – when I heard you messing about in the empty carriage.'

He paused, frowning. I quickly prompted him, to keep him talking.

'So what went wrong with Sir Dennis, Eric?'

'Something made him suspicious,' Eric said reluctantly. 'I had no trouble at all luring him into the unlit carriage; he was only too happy to assist a mere menial with a problem that was too big for him. I got behind Sir Dennis easily enough, but then he suddenly turned round and looked at me. He shouldn't have done that. He had no reason to do that! He saw me reaching for him, and he went for me. I couldn't believe it . . . a little weasel like him. Maybe getting so close to the important job he'd always wanted made him brave – or desperate.

'I had no choice but to put him in a choke hold and break his neck.' Eric smiled briefly. 'I took this self-defence course, you see, organized by the rail company. All the train staff had to take it, so we could learn to defend ourselves against angry passengers. Commuters can get really upset when they've been left standing in a stopped train for ages. Most of the staff treated the course as a laugh, but I took it seriously. And when they showed us the choke hold and told us to be very careful or we could break someone's neck . . . I remembered.

'After Sir Dennis was dead, I had to think quickly. Like you said, there was no way I could pass off a broken neck as an accident.'

'So you arranged the body on the toilet,' I said, keeping Eric's attention fixed on me. 'To confuse us as to when he died, and make it look as if he'd been murdered in a room locked from the inside. Classic murder mystery stuff. You moved suspicion away from yourself by banging loudly on the toilet door. You knew someone would be bound to come out from First Class, to see what was going on.'

'I thought it would be the bodyguard,' said Eric. 'And he didn't look smart enough to make any trouble. But, of course, I didn't know about you.'

'I thought you looked a little surprised when I was the one who appeared to see what was happening,' I said. 'But you went straight into your act anyway, pretending you'd only just arrived and that you were worried because Sir Dennis had been in the toilet for so long. And then you made up the story of the darkened carriage being locked and guarded, so that I'd fix my suspicions on the passengers in First Class. Hoping that would keep me occupied all the way to Bath. But the only way you could show me what had happened to Sir Dennis was to use your remote control to unlock the toilet door. And that was what gave you away.'

'That's what happens when you have to improvise,' said Eric.

'I have to ask, Eric,' I said carefully. 'Since you didn't know Sir Dennis, why did you agree to kill a complete stranger for some secret group you'd probably never even heard of?'

'For the money, of course,' said Eric. 'The rail company has been talking about getting rid of guards on trains, and I'm too old to find another job.'

'Who hired you?' I said.

'You'll never know,' said Eric.

'Excuse me,' said Penny. 'Can I ask a question?'

Eric looked at her, startled, as though he'd forgotten she was there.

'What?'

'Why did you tell the tea lady what had happened to Sir Dennis and then let her through?'

Eric seemed honestly stumped for a moment, thrown by a question he hadn't been expecting.

'Because she made such an effort to get it out of me. And because I thought it would be funny.'

'But why did you kill her afterwards?' said Penny.

He smiled at her. 'I had no choice. She came back from her little visit to First Class all fired up about Sir Dennis's murder. She told me she was actually a private detective working undercover and started firing all sorts of questions at me. I couldn't have that, so I just chose my moment carefully, caught her by surprise and broke her neck, like I did with Sir Dennis. Then all I had to do was use my remote control to open an exterior door and throw her body off the train.'

'But why leave her trolley in the deserted carriage?' I said.

His smile became a sneer. 'As a distraction, of course. While you were thinking about that, and about her, you wouldn't be thinking about me.'

I eased forward a step, and Penny hurried to come up with another question to hold Eric's attention.

'When you put out the lights in the next carriage, weren't you worried people would start asking questions?'

Eric actually smirked. 'These carriages are so ancient they're always having problems. None of the passengers even questioned me when I told them the lights wouldn't be coming back on again. No one ever questions a guard.'

He stood up a little straighter and smiled mockingly at everyone.

'Enough talking. It's time to put an end to this. When we finally roll into Bath and they open up this carriage, all they're going to find in First Class is a whole bunch of dead bodies, to add to the mystery of Sir Dennis being murdered in a toilet locked from the inside. Not quite the result my employers were hoping for, but it should be humiliating enough for Sir Dennis to suit them. And I'll just get off the train with the rest of the staff and walk away . . . to my all-expenses-paid retirement.'

He pushed Penny away from him. She stumbled forward, caught off balance, and I moved quickly to grab her and put her behind me, shielding her body with mine. Eric smiled at me. His eyes were bright and he was grinning broadly. This was his moment, and he was loving every bit of it.

'Can't afford to get her blood on me. They might notice that in Bath. Don't any of you think about trying to jump me! I still have an ace up my sleeve. You were right, Mr Jones, I'm not a professional. Not like you. But I still have something you don't.'

He reached inside his jacket with his free hand and pulled out the remote control. He hit a button and all the lights in the carriage went out.

It was immediately pitch-black, with not even a glimmer of light coming in through the windows. The passengers cried out in shock and fear. Unlike them, though, I could see in the dark. I could make out Eric, standing perfectly still, completely at home in the dark and happily savouring what he was going to do next. He didn't need to see us, to kill us. He knew where we were. I pushed Penny away from me, and she made a startled sound as she fell backwards. Eric immediately turned his gun in that direction, but I was already surging forward inhumanly quickly. I slammed into him, forcing his gun hand up and driving him back. He managed to get off one shot, but only into the carriage roof.

And then a sudden blast of light filled the carriage, dazzling both of us. Eric seized the moment to throw me off him, and I fell backwards, sprawling on the floor. Sita was standing in the aisle. Somehow she'd found one of the carriage's emergency flares and ignited it. The fierce green light filled the carriage. Eric aimed his gun at Sita. Brian threw himself forward, putting himself between Sita and the gun. Eric laughed breathlessly and shot him. The impact threw Brian back against Sita, and they both sat down hard on the floor. Sita dropped the flare and it rolled down the aisle, the green light jumping and flashing.

Rupert and Howard were both on their feet and heading for Eric. He aimed his gun at Howard, to shoot him at point-blank range. Rupert slammed into Howard, knocking him to one side and out of the line of fire. Eric aimed at Rupert, who froze.

Penny yelled Eric's name as she came charging down the aisle. Eric turned his gun on her. I forced myself up on to my feet and moved to put my body between Penny and Eric, readying myself for one last desperate lunge, while knowing even with my speed it wouldn't be enough to get to him in time. But I had to try, because I couldn't let anything happen to Penny. Eric aimed his gun at me, his finger tightening on the trigger. And Penny darted past me and hit Eric square in the nuts with her rolled-up copy of the *Fortean Times* before he could switch his aim to her.

All of Eric's breath shot out of him in a pained gasp, and he sank to his knees. I was quickly there to grab the gun from his hand. I hit Eric over the head with it, in just the right spot, and he fell forward on to his face and took no further interest in the proceedings. I knelt down beside him, prised the remote control out of his hand and turned the carriage lights back on.

I looked to where Sita was kneeling beside Brian, pressing a folded handkerchief against a bloody wound in his side.

'Hold that in place,' she said. 'I know it must hurt like hell, but a wound there isn't going to kill you.'

'What do you know about gunshot wounds?' said Brian. All the colour had drained out of his face, which was beaded with sweat, but he kept his voice steady.

'My dad's an army officer.'

'I should have known.'

'How did you know where to find the emergency flare?' said Brian.

'I did my research before I got on this train. First rule of the journalist: know what you're getting into. I put it in my pocket earlier, to use if the killer came after me.'

'Good thinking,' said Brian.

'Why did you risk your life to protect me?' said Sita.

'It's the job,' said Brian.

'Not because you fancied me?'

'Well, maybe that, too.'

'You'll last till we get to Bath,' said Sita. 'And then I'd better get a decent interview out of you.'

'I can do that,' said Brian.

They shared a smile.

I turned to Penny, who brandished her rolled-up magazine triumphantly.

'I saw that in a movie once. Always wanted to try it.'

'Nice timing,' I said.

And then the carriage slowed down in a series of jolts as the train finally pulled into Bath Spa station, right on time.

SEVEN

All Kinds of Loose Ends Taken Care Of

Carriage doors banged open the whole length of the train, and the flat heavy sounds ricocheted across Bath Spa station like a series of gunshots as the passengers disembarked. I got out of the First-Class carriage, took a quick look around, and then helped Penny down on to the platform. We both stretched slowly and leaned on each other. It had been a tiring journey and a difficult case, and it had taken a lot out of both of us. We moved away from the train and watched the passengers stream across the platform to the stairs that would lead them down to the station exits. They didn't look around much, intent on completing the last part of their journey as quickly as possible.

The train's arrival at Bath felt almost anti-climactic. There were no authorities waiting to meet us after all; no police or military or security . . . and no media scrum, either. There weren't even any family or loved ones waiting to greet the arriving passengers, or anyone standing around for the next train. Even as I thought that, a recorded voice announced there would be no more trains that evening and that the station would be closing in twenty minutes. I watched the last of the passengers disappear down the stairs, not even sparing a glance back over their shoulders for the train they'd just left. No reason why they should; for them, it had been just another journey. They had no idea of all the dramas that had taken place, in and around the First-Class carriage.

A restful quiet fell across the platform, broken only by the murmur of a gusting wind. Penny and I were left standing alone, wondering what we were supposed to do next. The night sky was very dark, with only a sliver of moon, and the air was bitterly cold. Penny huddled up against me, and I put my arm around her.

'I told you we should have brought our heavy coats,' she said.

'So you did.'

'What are we waiting for, Ishmael?'

'I was sure someone would be here to meet us,' I said. 'The new Head of the Psychic Weapons Division was murdered on our watch. All right, we caught the killer, but that wasn't the mission. We were supposed to keep Sir Dennis alive. Someone should have turned up, if only to take the body away.'

'Perhaps no one knows he's dead yet,' said Penny.

'The psychics watching over the train must know.'

And that was when four uniformed paramedics emerged from the stairwell, carrying two stretchers, and passed us by without a second glance. They headed straight for First Class, manoeuvred their stretchers through the open door and disappeared inside. Penny smiled at me.

'Somebody knows . . .'

There was a long pause, and then two of the paramedics reappeared, bringing Brian out on a stretcher. Sita came with him, holding Brian's hand all the way and talking to him reassuringly. He smiled at her, and she smiled at him.

'The things some people will do,' I said, 'for an exclusive interview.'

'Oh, hush,' said Penny. 'I think it's very sweet.'

Brian and Sita had only just disappeared down the stairs when the other two paramedics emerged from First Class, carrying Eric on a stretcher. Unlike Brian, Eric was held in place by stout leather straps, almost certainly not for his health. He looked surprisingly resigned about it all. His eyes caught mine for a moment, but he looked away without saying anything. The paramedics had nothing to say either. They disappeared down the stairs and were passed on their way by the Colonel coming up. He was wearing a heavy military coat against the cold of the night, and his homburg hat was tilted at what he probably considered a rakish angle.

'What the hell is he doing here?' Penny said quietly.

'He knows Sir Dennis is dead,' I said. 'That's why there are no authorities and no media presence.'

'Do you think we're in trouble?' said Penny.

'Look at the man,' I said. 'Does he have the air of someone coming to compliment us on a job well done? No, we screwed up, and the Colonel is here to tell us just how deep in it we are.'

'But who told him?'

'I'm guessing the Division,' I said. 'Which would suggest there's a lot more to this situation than we were told.'

'We caught the murderer,' said Penny. 'That should count for something.'

'Yes,' I said, 'it should.'

The Colonel strode over to join us and managed a frosty smile.

'You don't normally hand your prisoners over in such a state they have to be stretchered away.'

'That was Penny,' I said.

She smiled dazzlingly at the Colonel, who seemed genuinely lost for words. And then we all looked round as a door slammed open in First Class, and Rupert and Howard stepped out on to the platform. They stayed where they were, looking carefully around to make sure everyone else had gone. I moved quickly back to join them, and they both managed a smile for me.

'We wanted to avoid any reporters,' said Rupert. 'But it would seem there aren't any.'

'What are we supposed to do now?' said Howard, glancing at the Colonel, who was busy talking to Penny and studiously ignoring us.

'As far as I'm concerned, you're free to go,' I said. 'The drama is over, and the players depart.'

'Your drama might be,' said Rupert. 'That private detective masquerading as a tea lady said there'd be someone waiting outside the station to follow me wherever I go. You're someone in authority, Mr Jones; can't you do something?'

'I'm afraid not,' I said. 'At least now you know what's going on. In the end, it's your wife . . . and your life. You have to make up your own mind as to what you're going to do with them.'

Rupert nodded slowly. 'I have to be who I am, and to hell

with the consequences. If Julia wants a divorce, she can have one. And if she's determined to keep all the money . . . she can have that too. I never cared about it, although I never could convince her of that. The only thing that really matters is that I have to be true to myself.'

'I know what you mean,' I said.

'Do you?' said Rupert. He looked at me searchingly. 'Well . . . perhaps you do.'

I turned to Howard, who met my gaze steadily.

'What about you?' I said bluntly. 'Are you still determined to kill yourself? It's not too late to find some new reason to go on living.'

Howard surprised me with something very like a real smile. 'A funny thing happened when the guard nearly killed me, and Rupert risked his own life to save mine. I suddenly realized that I did want to live after all. It seems life can still surprise me.' He turned to Rupert. 'I could use a drink. Perhaps you'd care to join me. There must be somewhere around here still open. And then we can keep an eye out for whoever might be following you – and take turns kicking their arse.'

'Sounds like a plan to me,' said Rupert.

They walked away, chatting companionably, and descended the stairs together. I went back to join Penny and the Colonel.

'You really think we should just let them go?' said Penny. 'With all the problems they're facing?'

'What else can we do?' I said reasonably. 'I can solve mysteries and catch killers, but I can't live people's lives for them. I have enough trouble living my own. Have faith in them, Penny. People often turn out to be stronger than they appear.'

I turned to the Colonel, ready to explain what had happened to Sir Dennis, but he stopped me with a raised hand.

'I know everything that happened on the train,' he said calmly. 'The Division psychics gave me a complete report. Downloaded the damned thing right into my head. Good thing I wasn't driving at the time.'

'I allowed Sir Dennis to be killed,' I said. 'Sorry about that.'

'Don't be,' the Colonel said briskly. 'He's no great loss.'

'But he was going to be Head of the Psychic Weapons Division!' said Penny.

The Colonel smiled. 'Sir Dennis was never going to take over the British Psychic Weapons Division. He was just a minor politician, put in place to act as a decoy, while I escorted the real head on a separate train. He is currently safely ensconced at Bath MOD Headquarters, being briefed on his new duties.'

'You acted as bodyguard for the new head?' I said.

'Exactly,' said the Colonel. 'While Division psychics watched over us from a distance, of course.'

'Of course,' I said. 'But since when have you lowered yourself to do actual work in the field?'

'Since the Division asked the Organization to provide a reliable man, and the Organization chose me,' said the Colonel. 'I took it as a compliment. And it's not like I expected to have to do anything, as long as you two did your job properly and kept everyone else convinced Sir Dennis was the new head.'

'Then the Division and the Organization were working together from the beginning?' I said.

'Of course,' said the Colonel. 'You can't keep anything from psychics.'

'Sir Dennis didn't know he was a decoy,' I said. 'He thought he'd got the job for real.'

'It was vital he believed that,' the Colonel said patiently. 'So the enemy psychics would believe he was the real deal. And, of course, you being there as his bodyguards helped to confirm that.'

'But how could a man like Sir Dennis honestly believe he'd been awarded such an important position?' said Penny.

'He was led to believe that the role amounted to little more than that of a prestigious figurehead,' said the Colonel. 'Payment for past favours, and his continued silence about them. He believed the job was real because he wanted it to be real.' The Colonel allowed himself a brief cold smile.

'So he was just bait in a trap,' I said.

'Exactly,' said the Colonel.

'Along with us,' said Penny.

'That's the job, sometimes,' said the Colonel.

'Who is the new Head of Division?' I said. 'Would we have heard of him?'

'You don't need to know that,' said the Colonel.

'Why did I just know you were going to say that?' said Penny.

'Perhaps you're psychic,' said the Colonel.

'So we didn't actually fail in our mission,' I said. 'Because protecting Sir Dennis never was the mission. The real Head is safe, and we caught the assassin. Which is really what we were there for.'

'That's an acceptable way of looking at it,' said the Colonel.

Penny looked across at the stairs. 'Those paramedics aren't taking Eric to a hospital, are they?'

'Hardly,' said the Colonel. 'Mr Holder is currently on his way to a very secure location, where the Division's top people are waiting to dig his employers' identity out of his head.'

'Won't the people who hired Eric have anticipated that?' I said. 'They're bound to have placed telepathic blocks in his mind, to hide who they were. Assuming they ever told Eric who they really were.'

'The Division has a number of very experienced people who are very good at getting to the truth,' said the Colonel. 'I'm sure Mr Holder knows all kinds of things he doesn't know he knows, which will provide numerous useful leads.'

'Do you have any idea who was behind this?' I said.

The Colonel shrugged. 'Could be any number of foreign powers, or interested parties, looking for a chance to throw a stone into the pond and see how far the ripples would spread.'

'These psychics . . . they won't hurt Eric, will they?' said Penny. 'I mean . . .'

'Torture?' said the Colonel. 'Nothing so crude. They'll just slip into his mind and help him see the error of his ways, until they have him eating out of their hands and only too eager to tell them everything. They might even persuade him to work for the Division, as a double agent.'

'So he's never going to face justice?' I said. 'For the murders of Sir Dennis and Dee, or for trying to kill the rest of us?'

'I don't think that's in anyone's best interests, do you?' said the Colonel. 'It's not like we could put him on a witness stand. Or you, for that matter.'

I had to nod. Penny didn't look at all happy, but she didn't say anything.

'I'm sure the Division will get good work out of Mr Holder,' the Colonel said calmly. 'For as long as he lasts.'

Penny shuddered briefly as the implications of that struck home. But I was remembering Eric's gun pressed against her head and I really couldn't find it in me to feel sorry for him.

'I think it's best that all of this is forgotten as quickly as possible,' the Colonel said briskly. 'Just one small victory in the secret wars that take place every day, which the general public never gets to hear about.'

'Why was Sir Dennis chosen as bait?' said Penny.

'Because he'd been a bad boy,' said the Colonel. 'Got caught with his hand in the cookie jar once too often. That's politics for you: red in tooth and claw. But I really wouldn't feel sorry for him. I've seen that man's file. If you knew half the things he did and got away with, his death wouldn't bother you in the least. The world is a better place for him not being in it.'

'And now that he's safely dead,' I said, 'he can't talk about all the favours he did for people currently in high positions. No doubt they'll all feel a lot safer, once the news breaks . . .'

I was careful not to sound too accusing, but the Colonel had no trouble picking up on my implication.

'I wouldn't be too sure about that. Apparently, the Division psychics took a good look inside Sir Dennis's head while they were watching over the train. I'm sure they found all kinds of interesting things in there.'

I looked at him sharply. 'Is that how the Division ensures its independence from political interference? By knowing things about people in power?'

'I couldn't possibly comment,' said the Colonel.

'What about the other people travelling with us in First Class?' said Penny. 'Rupert and Howard, Sita and Brian?'

'What about them?' said the Colonel.

'They had no idea of the danger they were in,' I said. 'They didn't agree to be a part of this.'

'They were a necessary part of the camouflage,' said the Colonel.

'Then can we at least leave them alone now, to get on with their lives?' I said. 'It's not like they know anything that matters.'

'They've been put through enough,' said Penny.

The Colonel pursed his lips for a moment. 'I don't see any need to detain them. I've been told the Division psychics will only take a quick peek inside their heads, from a distance. I'm sure if they do happen across something that shouldn't be there, they'll just quietly delete it.'

And then we all looked round, at the sound of a door opening in the First-Class carriage. A single figure stepped carefully down on to the platform and closed the door behind him. It was the psychic Penny and I had met in the Hipster Bar at Paddington. The man called Nemo – Mr Nobody. I stared at him blankly as he came strolling over to join us, and then I turned to look accusingly at the Colonel, who didn't appear in the least surprised. Nemo stopped before us and nodded courteously.

'Yes,' he said. 'I was there all along, hidden behind an invisible shield, observing everything.'

'You were right there in the carriage with us?' said Penny. 'All the way from Paddington?'

'Yes,' said Nemo.

'But I didn't see you!' I said.

'No one ever does, unless I allow them to,' said Nemo. 'That's part of my job description.'

'But . . . there weren't any of the usual signs,' I said. 'No psychic fallout!'

'I can suppress that kind of thing, when necessary,' Nemo said patiently. 'Just as I did at Paddington.'

I felt like saying a great many things, but given that Nemo probably already knew what I was thinking, I didn't see the point. Penny still saw the warning signs in my face and cut in quickly.

'Why didn't you reveal yourself, once Sir Dennis had been killed? You could have probed the minds of everyone in First Class, and saved us wasting all that time interrogating them!'

'And why didn't you intervene when Eric was threatening to kill us all?' I said, just a bit heatedly.

'I was under strict orders not to give my presence away,' said Nemo. 'I was only there to be the last line of defence, in the event that the Division psychics watching over the train failed. Sir Dennis's murder caught me completely by surprise, because I was only watching for a psychic attack. But I had complete faith in the two of you to catch the killer. And to deal with any other little problems that might arise. Think of me as the safety net you didn't need. Now, if you'll excuse me, I must be off to MOD Headquarters.'

He smiled at each of us and then walked unhurriedly over to the stairs. I turned to the Colonel. He shrugged.

'Division field agents are a law unto themselves and go their own way. Remind you of anyone?'

Penny dragged the conversation determinedly back to where it had been before we were interrupted.

'Those psychics who'll be digging into Rupert's and Howard's minds – could they do anything to help them? Like keep Howard from killing himself?'

She started to explain, but the Colonel stopped her with a raised hand. 'My briefing covered everyone in First Class. But there's a limit to what psychics can do, without brain-washing people. In the end, we are all the captains of our own souls and must make our own decisions. The best a psychic could do would be to give Howard a nudge in the right direction and hope for the best.'

'But will they?' I said.

'I don't see why not,' said the Colonel. 'As you said, these people didn't ask to be part of our little game. An argument could be made that we owe them something.'

'What about Rupert?' I said.

'Mr Hall's life is his own business,' said the Colonel. 'We exist to protect people from outside threats, not meddle in their private lives.'

'Could Sita still have an exclusive for her paper?' I said.

'I don't see why not,' said the Colonel. 'In fact, carefully managed, that could make a good distraction to help us hide what really happened to Sir Dennis.'

I couldn't keep from smiling. Sita would really hate that if she ever found out.

'What about Brian?' said Penny. 'None of what happened was his fault.'

'I'm sure he'll receive some kind of commendation for being wounded in the line of duty,' said the Colonel. 'Now, is there anything else? I do have a report to write before I can put this evening behind me.'

I looked back at the train as a thought struck me. 'What about Sir Dennis's body? We can't just leave it there.'

'It's already gone,' said the Colonel.

'I didn't see anything!' I said.

The Colonel smiled. 'That's psychics for you.'

'The sneaky bastards!' said Penny.

'Well, quite,' said the Colonel. He looked at me thoughtfully. 'Since you did perform a valuable service this evening, for the Division as well as the Organization, Mr Nemo has performed a small service for you, Mr Jones. I'm told he couldn't read your mind, which came as something of a surprise to him, but he was able to help you remember something you'd forgotten. The memory should reappear in your mind any time now. So, until we meet again . . .'

He tipped his homburg to Penny and to me, and then strode briskly away and off down the stairs. We watched carefully till we were sure he was gone, and then looked at each other.

'We'd better find a hotel in Bath and travel back to London tomorrow,' said Penny. 'What was all that about you forgetting something?'

'Damned if I know,' I said. 'I suppose it's some comfort that even if I couldn't detect Nemo's presence, at least he couldn't read my mind.'

And then I broke off and looked at Penny, shocked and startled.

'I've just remembered! I wasn't the only member of my crew to survive the starship crash! There was another . . .'